"We did it!"

Cal was going to give ... arms and the feisty woman trudging behind him.

He turned his head again. Snow clung to Abby's dark hair, and she looked almost fragile against the desolate landscape. As if reading his thoughts, she lifted her head and caught his stare.

She was just as tough as he was. Which he knew already.

Wait! He froze. What was that? The low hum of an approaching vehicle caught his ear.

"Abby! Quick! We need to take cover!"

"What?"

"Cover! Now!" He grabbed her hand and pulled her toward the side of the embankment. Would the driver notice their footprints? No. The gusting wind had already dusted the tarmac with enough snow to cover their tracks.

He handed Abby the baby and crouched down beside her.

"Ricky," she whispered. The word was like a dagger in the cold night air.

His free hand dug into the snow and searched for something, *anything*, he could use as a weapon...

Jaycee Bullard was born and raised in the great state of Minnesota, the fourth child in a family of five. Growing up, she loved to read, especially books by Astrid Lindgren and Georgette Heyer. In the ten years since graduating with a degree in classical languages, she has worked as a paralegal and an office manager, before finally finding her true calling as a preschool Montessori teacher and as a writer of romantic suspense.

Books by Jaycee Bullard

Love Inspired Suspense

Framed for Christmas
Fatal Ranch Reunion
Rescue on the Run

Visit the Author Profile page at Harlequin.com.

RESCUE ON THE RUN

JAYCEE BULLARD

LOVE INSPIRED SUSPENSE
INSPIRATIONAL ROMANCE

If you purchased this book without a cover you should be aware that this book is stolen property. It was reported as "unsold and destroyed" to the publisher, and neither the author nor the publisher has received any payment for this "stripped book."

LOVE INSPIRED® SUSPENSE
INSPIRATIONAL ROMANCE

Recycling programs for this product may not exist in your area.

ISBN-13: 978-1-335-55454-3

Rescue on the Run

Copyright © 2021 by Jean Bullard

All rights reserved. No part of this book may be used or reproduced in any manner whatsoever without written permission except in the case of brief quotations embodied in critical articles and reviews.

This is a work of fiction. Names, characters, places and incidents are either the product of the author's imagination or are used fictitiously. Any resemblance to actual persons, living or dead, businesses, companies, events or locales is entirely coincidental.

This edition published by arrangement with Harlequin Books S.A.

For questions and comments about the quality of this book, please contact us at CustomerService@Harlequin.com.

Love Inspired
22 Adelaide St. West, 40th Floor
Toronto, Ontario M5H 4E3, Canada
www.Harlequin.com

Printed in U.S.A.

Be careful for nothing;
but in every thing by prayer and supplication with
thanksgiving let your requests be made known unto God.
And the peace of God, which passeth all understanding,
shall keep your hearts and minds through Christ Jesus.
—*Philippians* 4:6–7

To Noah and Mae.
You were the miracles and highlights of the last year.

To my sister Clare.
You believed in this story from the very first draft.

To the residents of Parkshore Senior Campus.
Thank you for your interest and support for my writing.
I miss visiting you more than I can say.
Know that you are in my thoughts and prayers.

ONE

All day long, a stiff west wind had been swirling together the worst of January weather—snow and sleet and damp cold. Winter in North Dakota. Time for curling up by the fire with a good book and a warm cup of tea. Not for standing in front of the locked doors of Keystone Bank, hands clenched into tight fists.

Abby Marshall had just about decided to give up on waiting and head for home when her cell pulsed against her hip. She fished it out of her pocket and checked the screen.

Department of Children and Family Services. Her heartbeat quickened. It had to be her social worker, calling with news about the adoption. She fumbled with her gloves as footsteps crunched on the path behind her.

"Have they closed already? It's not even five."

The voice was familiar, and so was the oversize boot planted next to her on the stoop. Both belonged to Cal Stanek, Sheriff of Dagger Lake County, and, according to some, the best-looking bachelor in the tristate area.

An uncomfortable silence passed between them. Almost from the day Cal arrived in town, well-meaning friends and acquaintances had been trying to set the two of them up. Which made it awkward whenever she and Cal ran into each other at city hall or the bank or the checkout at the market. It didn't help that, beneath a façade of cheerful indifference, the sheriff often seemed to be sizing her up through narrowed, vaguely disapproving eyes.

There was always that moment when it felt like they ought to be able to move beyond the usual pleasantries, grab a cup of coffee and have a collegial conversation about their jobs and life in Dagger Lake. But from the look of Cal's attire—ice fishing overalls and bulky wool coat—as well as the anxious expression on his face, that talk wasn't going to happen today.

"What's going on? Why's the door locked?" Cal's voice brought her back to the present, and she stepped sideways to get out of his way. Their elbows bumped, and her cell slipped from her grasp and disappeared into a pile of deep, wet snow.

No! She needed to answer that call. If Davey was coming to live with her, there wasn't a moment to spare. She dropped to her knees and began to dig, clawing through the slush until her fingers closed around a rectangular object. Her phone, dripping wet, with moisture already seeping through the casing. She pushed herself up, her thumb frantically pressing the power button, but the screen remained blank. She tried again. Nothing.

Cal reached across the stoop and swiped a sleeve against the phone's screen. "If you power it off and wait a few minutes, it might still work. Look," he said, tilting his head downward. "I think I see something inside on the floor."

As Cal pressed his face against the window that framed the bank's threshold, she rechecked her cell. Fuzzy gray lines now crisscrossed the screen, but there was still no reception. How long would she have to wait to find out if the folks at Children and Family Services had approved her application? She tamped down her frustration. Maybe there was a landline she could use in the lobby. Her eyes darted back toward Cal. That was when she noticed the look on his face. Assessing and hard. Tracking the downward direction of his glance, she saw what she had missed on her first peek through the glass—the body of a man lying facedown on the floor, a wide circle of blood pooled beneath his head. Given the navy blue uniform and the thin, gray hair, she assumed that the injured man was Zander Phillips, the weekend security guard at the bank.

"Oh no." She bit back the scream that was lodged in her throat.

Cal pressed a finger to his lips and motioned for her to step away.

She moved toward the spot by the side of the building where he stood waiting.

"What's going on?"

Cal's face was grim. "It looks like we stumbled into the middle of a robbery."

"What about Zander? Do you think he's dead?"

"Not sure. But it doesn't look good."

Her mind switched into paramedic gear. "If we could

break a window and get inside, I might be able to help him."

"No, Abby. At this point, it's not safe. The fact that there are so many cars in the lot makes me think that the robbers are still in the building. More than one shooter could be inside, holding other hostages. We need to get backup here right away." He reached into the pocket of his overalls and pulled out a set of keys. "Here. Take these. My truck is parked in the lot. And my phone is in the cupholder between the seats. The code is five-five-seven-two. Call nine-one-one and tell the operator to send as many deputies as she can muster."

"Five-five-seven-two," she repeated, her heart pounding in her chest. As Cal pulled his Glock from the holster under his coat, she swallowed hard. "I can do that. But what about you?"

"I'm going to do a recon of the outside of the building. The more I can learn about the situation, the better it will be when backup arrives."

She ignored the rest of the questions crowding her brain. All she could think about was Zander. Minutes, even seconds, could decide if he lived or died. But Cal was right. The best course of action was to call for help. Once the 911 operator passed the message to the proper authorities, it wouldn't be long before deputies arrived on the scene, armed with weapons and shields. The team on the ambulance would be right behind them, well prepared to do everything they could to handle the medical emergency. The bank robbers would be apprehended. And the hostages would be safe.

But before any of that could happen, she needed to

find Cal's truck. She retraced her steps along the path, stopping at the curb to look for his familiar blue F-150. Bits of frozen ice pelted her face as she struggled to discern the contours of the snow-covered vehicles scattered haphazardly across the lot. It was already getting dark, and a green-gray dusk shrouded her vision. She raised her hand to shield her eyes and peered out through a veil of falling snow. Yes! There it was, a dusting of flakes already covering the truck bed and the side windows. She ran across the lot, skidding through the slush as wetness seeped through the soles of her shoes.

She pressed the button on the key fob. The horn honked, the taillights flashed and the locks disengaged.

Pulling herself up into the driver's seat, she slammed the door shut behind her. She took a deep breath and brushed the snow from her shoulders. Inside the cab, the frosted windows bathed the space in a tomb-like glow, making it hard to see more than a few inches in front of her. Cal had said that his phone was in the cupholder, but—her fingers clenched from the cold as she raked her hand across the console—it didn't seem to be there.

She flicked on the overhead light and scanned the cab. The charger was empty. Where was the phone?

Desperation guided her senses as she pried her hands into the sides of both seats. But there was nothing there, except for a pack of mints and a broken pen.

Had Cal been confused with his directions? Maybe he'd made a mistake and left his cell at home. She shook her head. That wasn't likely. It had to be somewhere in the truck. It had probably slid off the console and lodged under the seat.

The beam on the ceiling flickered and dimmed. It was still so dark inside the cab. She pressed the key into the truck's ignition, and the light blinked back on as the motor responded with a dull roar. It was tempting to put the truck in gear and head into town. She might have to do that if she couldn't find the phone. But with Zander bleeding out on the floor of the bank, every second was precious.

Her breath came out in short bursts, forming a thin cloud of condensation on the windows. As she flicked on the defroster, her eyes raced across the dashboard, searching for the knob that controlled the wipers. The one in her car was to the left of the gearshift, but the F-150's was on the turn signal.

She rotated the dial.

A green arrow began to blink. She twisted the notch underneath it. There was a moment of hesitation before the blades engaged, but it took only one pass for the wipers to clear the snow from the glass, making it easier to see.

But the phone was nowhere to be found. Leaning over the headrest, she checked the back seat. And there it was, laying upside down on the floor. She stretched her arms to pick it up and then slid back down on the seat.

Her legs were shaking as she set the phone on her lap. What was the code again? Five-five-seven-two. She had just punched in the last of the four digits when the click of a handle being pushed and released sent a shock wave of tension straight up her spine.

"Cal?" she said.

Not Cal.

She froze for a second as the side door flew open, and a dark-haired woman with a gun pulled herself into the passenger seat. "Don't move," the woman said.

She couldn't if she wanted to. A cloud of fear fogged her brain as she stared at the pistol aimed at her chest. Her heart seemed to stop, and then it began to drum frantically. But she couldn't allow herself to lose her nerve. Her eyes slid sideways, and a germ of an idea took root in her brain. The console between the seats was high enough to shield the lower part of her body. Which meant that the woman sitting next to her couldn't see the phone.

The hairs on the back of her neck prickled in anticipation. She could feel the woman's eyes on her as she reached down toward the cell and silenced the volume. With the tip of her thumb, she skimmed the call icon. For the beat of one second, her finger remained poised against the glass, waiting to slide across the numbers on the screen.

Nine…one…

A sharp object nudged against her ribs. Her hand froze as the woman pressed the barrel of the pistol hard against her chest.

"What is it about 'don't move' that you don't understand?"

Cal kept his head down as he crept past the low-lying evergreens along the north side of the building. Under normal circumstances, he would settle into a safe spot and wait for backup. But given the unknowns of the situation, he couldn't remain still. The threat of hostages was a very real possibility. He glanced down at his watch. Any minute now, Abby would be dialing 911.

According to protocol, the message would be passed to the deputy manning the desk at the sheriff's department, and every available officer in the area would be sent to the scene.

And when they arrived, they'd be grateful for a solid recon of the site.

He reached the corner of the lot and made the turn toward the back of the building. The snow was coming down harder now, obscuring any footprints along the path. His mind scrambled to imagine every possible scenario to explain what might have happened in the lobby of the bank. How many civilians had been inside? How many robbers? Why hadn't the teller on duty pushed the emergency button to notify the police? He couldn't be sure, but Zander Phillips probably never had a chance. The guard's gun was still in his holster when his body hit the floor.

He could only speculate about the events that followed. Any remaining hostages would have been taken at gunpoint to a back room as the robbers—based on past experience, there had to be at least two, maybe three—emptied the cash from the drawers. Breaking into the safe would be their next step. Which explained why the lobby was deserted when he and Abby arrived at the door.

Frustration gnawed at his senses. How had he failed to realize that something was wrong the moment he pulled into the parking lot? There were too many cars for closing time on a Saturday afternoon. He had noticed Abby's white Nissan as well as the late-model minivan and light blue Taurus that he had seen on previous visits. But the black SUV with tinted windows and out-of-state plates parked by the entrance should have raised his suspicions.

But no. He had walked right by it, lost in thought, already anticipating his upcoming weekend ice fishing with his dad, and far too distracted to put two and two together and realize something was wrong.

That had been a mistake.

Treading lightly along the path, he approached the security door on the west side of the building. He considered the layout of the bank as he planned his next move. The door opened into the hall next to the lobby, and its tempered steel construction would make it impossible to break through.

Of course, there was always the chance that the robbers had gotten careless. They had no reason to be expecting trouble so near to closing time on a Saturday afternoon.

Cal reached for the handle. He drew in a quick breath as it turned in his hand.

He stepped into the hall, his finger on the trigger of his Glock.

As the door swished shut behind him, a shot rang out, splintering the wall above him, well off the intended mark. It was followed by another blast from the opposite direction. That one was close. Too close.

He plastered his body against the smooth, cool surface of the pillar at the far end of the lobby and returned fire. His heart thudded as he did the calculations in his head. So far at least, there seemed to be only two shooters and no signs of hostages anywhere. From the trajectory of the bullets, it seemed that the younger gunman was lurking in the shadows along the front wall while the second shooter was crouched down behind the cashier's station in the back of the lobby.

It didn't take a genius to predict what would happen next.

One of the men would make a move, counting on the other to provide cover.

He held his Glock steady with both hands, blew out a long breath and peeked around the column. A rippling crack sliced through the air. He yanked his head back just in time as fine, gray grit rained down on his hair.

He wiped the dust from his face with his sleeve. Sweat beaded along his temples. Three more shots, and the pillar would be gone. He needed to relocate to a place where his exposure was limited. But crossing the room without drawing fire would be next to impossible. Already the robbers were fanning out on either side of him. In a matter of seconds, he would be outflanked. It was now or never. As he glanced back around the column, another bullet streaked by him, whistling inches from his head. But this time he was ready. He swiveled in the direction of the shooter and fired twice. Then he took off running.

Had any of his bullets hit their mark? He couldn't be sure. His only goal at the moment was making it across the lobby unscathed. He was almost there. Just a few feet to go. He stumbled sideways and rolled onto his back. Holding his gun in front of him, he pushed himself toward a table, knocking it sideways to form a barricade.

He took a steadying breath and prepared for round two. There were seven bullets left in his magazine. And an extra clip on his ankle holster. Plenty of ammo.

And if Abby had called for help, backup would be on the way.

He peered around the side of the table and took stock of his shooters' positions. One of the gunmen had barricaded himself behind the cashier's station. The other was lying on the floor, clutching a bloody hand to his chest. So he hadn't missed with his shot. From the way the fallen man was moaning, the injury appeared severe enough to count him out.

One down and one to go.

Cal pulled himself upright, his gun at the ready. He had a clear shot at the first gunman, and the chance to end this now.

But when he twisted his head, his stomach clenched. A tall woman was standing in front of the door he'd entered minutes ago, her brows bent into a deep frown as she pressed her pistol against Abby's head. Abby's eyes met his with a look of abject disappointment.

"Drop your weapon now," the woman said. "And kick it over to me."

Cal's finger froze on the trigger. He could probably still get off a shot. But as he looked at Abby, he knew the risk was too great. Her face was pale and drawn against her jet-black hair. But there was fire and determination blazing in her eyes.

He had run out of options. There was no other choice but to obey the woman's command.

Setting down his gun, he nudged it out of reach and raised his hands in surrender.

The younger of the shooters, a man in a black T-shirt, stepped around from the cashier's station. With a slow and steady gait, he walked across the lobby, the snarl on his lips daring Cal to move.

Cal's eyes didn't waver as he held the robber's taunting gaze.

Two steps closer, and the man was at his side. Without speaking a word, he raised his .44 Magnum and brought it down hard on the back of Cal's head.

And everything faded to black.

TWO

Abby bit back a scream as Cal's body crumpled to the floor. She glanced around the lobby, struggling to come to terms with the scene unfolding before her.

The place looked like a battle zone, with bits of wood and plaster and brass scattered across the floor. The mahogany desk had been upended. The deposit slips and notepaper that once filled its drawers were strewn on every surface like confetti caught in the wind. To her left, one of the robbers—an older man with a beard and a moustache—was propped up against the wall, clutching his hand and moaning with pain. The body of the security guard was still in front of the door, his eyes open and lifeless. Zander Phillips, husband, and father of three grown kids. Rest in peace.

"Well, hey, there, Martina. Looks like you were right about securing the outside of the building," the younger robber in a black T-shirt said. The sheath of a long thin knife swayed against his hip as he moved across the room. "I'll take care of Tomas while you take the hostage to the break room. We'll deal with this one later."

He nudged Cal's prone body with his boot. "Come back and help me move him. I want to clean up the lobby in case we have any more unexpected visitors."

Where would they move him? And was Cal seriously injured or just temporarily out of commission? She swiveled her head to check as the woman—Martina—pushed her forward toward the hall.

Abby's brain flashed to her next move. Should she try to break free and make a run for it? Her assailant had loosened her grip, and she sensed an opportunity. But would she be quick enough to make it out the door? And if she reached the parking lot, what then? The consequences of failure hung like the acrid smell of gunpowder lingering in the air.

Too late. Martina's long fingernails dug deep against the sleeve of her parka. Abby tried to go limp, but her assailant clamped down harder, pulling her into the corridor, dragging her past two closed doors until they reached a room at the end of the hall.

Martina pulled a key from her pocket and fitted it into the lock.

"Wait!" Abby turned to face her. "I'm a paramedic. And I'm worried about my friend, the tall man in the overalls who's still lying on the lobby floor. Can you bring him…?" The rest of her words caught in her throat as Martina slid her hand against the small of her back and shoved her across the threshold.

Abby's legs buckled under her as she landed hard on the carpeted floor. The door slammed shut behind her, plunging the room into darkness. She pushed up on her elbows and swiveled her head. Hot tears pricked at the backs of her eyes, but she blinked them away. She took a breath to calm her racing heart. The air felt warm as it filled up her lungs, and the quivering in her body began to slow down.

Calm, steadying breaths. Calm, steadying breaths. She refused to give in to panic. She was trained to deal with emergencies. At least once a week, she answered a call where a victim was in shock. It was all about turning negative emotions into a constructive response. She pulled herself upright and traced her hand along the wall until she found a switch. The overhead fluorescent fixture flickered twice, illuminating the windowless room in a dim yellow glow. She tried the door. Locked. No surprise there. Slipping her arms out of the sleeves of her parka, she kicked off her wet pumps and surveyed what looked to be a typical break room. In one corner, there was a refrigerator with an old-school television propped by its side. Next to that was a trestle table with four sling-back chairs.

The clock on the microwave flashed the time. Five thirty-two. It had been almost forty minutes since she arrived at the bank, and it was hopelessly apparent that help was not on the way. How different this would be if Davey was already living with her. If there was someone who might worry when she failed to arrive home as promised and call the police to report her missing.

Had she really just wished for something that existed only in her deepest imaginings? There was no child at home that needed minding, no worried babysitter to wonder why she hadn't returned. At least not yet. No one would miss her until Monday morning, when she was slotted to start her shift.

As her eyes grew acclimated to the dim light of the break room, she noticed what looked like a human form stretched out on a sofa by the back wall. What! Who? She rushed forward to investigate. Curled up under a light sheet was bank teller Isobel Carrolls. Nine months pregnant and asleep.

"Isobel?" Abby reached over and touched her arm. "Are you hurt in any way?"

Isobel opened her eyes and blinked. "No, but… What are you doing here, Abby? Do you know about the robbery? It was horrible. One of the men held a gun to my head and said if I moved, he would shoot me. Zander tried to help me. Is he okay?"

Abby shook her head.

"Oh, no," Isobel wailed. "He was so brave. Ohh." She gasped and clutched her sides. "My stomach aches so much." She rocked her body from side to side, her face tight with anguish. Her writhing lasted for a couple of minutes and then ended as suddenly as it began.

Could the bank teller be in the early stages of labor? Abby pulled in a long, deep breath. She knew from their time together in Bible Study that Isobel's baby was due any day. "How long have you been experiencing these pains?"

"Not too long. They started right after the robbers dragged me into the break room. I was screaming, and the older one said he would give me something to calm me down. He had a bottle of pills and forced a couple of them down my throat. I didn't want to take them, but he made me." She raised her head and pushed her tears away. "But everything must be okay since you're here now. Did the police catch the robbers? Can I go home?"

Regret and self-recriminations pitted in Abby's stomach. If only she hadn't wasted so much time searching for Cal's phone, she might have called 911 and help would be on the way. She shook her head. "I'm sorry to tell you this, but the robbers are still here. I'm a hostage just like you." She expected the look of disappointment that played across the bank teller's face, but not the way Isobel's entire body seemed to shudder as her head dropped back against the sofa.

"Iz. I'm really worried about your pains. Can you tell me how close together they are?"

The answer to the question came as a quiet snore. Apparently, her patient had fallen back to sleep.

Abby blew out a deep breath of frustration. It didn't make sense that Isobel would choose to nap at a time like this. Unless… Isobel had said that one of the robbers had forced her to take some tablets. Had she been given sleeping pills to calm her hysterics? That wouldn't be advisable for someone in her condition. Especially if she actually was in labor, which could easily have been jump-started by the trauma of the robbery. These kinds of early warning pains could last for hours, sometimes even days. But it was impossible to predict which would be the case.

Either way, she needed to get Isobel out of here—and fast.

Pacing across the floor, she considered what she remembered about the building's layout. When Keystone

Bank opened its doors in the eighties, its unique A-frame design had made it a landmark in Dagger Lake. But the decade had passed, and its architecture had become dated. In recent years, the ceiling in the lobby had been opened up to provide a brighter, more open space. But the offices in the back occupied the dark and windowless part of the original structure. Which meant that she and Isobel were stuck in a room with only one point of exit—a locked door.

From the hall came the soft slide of rubber soles against a tile floor. Was it Martina—or one of the others—returning to kill the hostages? She needed to act while she had the chance. If she could overpower the person who opened the door, she could run to the lobby and phone for help.

Her shoulders tightened, and the hairs on the nape of her neck lifted in fear. There was no time for a well-thought-out strategy. She crouched down to search for a weapon, something, anything she could use against her assailant. Under the counter, she found a heavy metal tray. She grabbed it and took a position along the wall. Raising her weapon above her head, she waited as the handle turned. The door swung open, and the man in the black T-shirt stepped inside.

Abby didn't hesitate. With a hard swing, she brought the tray down on his head.

"Ugh!" Black T-shirt dropped with a thunk the load he was carrying, and staggered forward, his face a mask of twisted fury and pain.

Pinpricks of fear danced down Abby's spine. It had been a mistake to think that a man of his size would be disabled by a blow to the head. She hadn't hit him hard enough to knock him out. All she had succeeded in doing was inflaming his anger and raising the stakes. He flung himself at her, his eyes murderous as he pushed backward, slapping her face until the sting of his fingers burned against her flesh. Her legs bowed beneath her, and she crumpled to the ground. Instinct guided her actions as she pulled her knees up against her chest and backed into the corner. Her entire body trembled with terror as he moved toward her, the long edge of a knife glimmering in his hand. Her stomach roiled as he bent down and pressed the blade against her neck. It bit into her skin, and the sticky sensation of blood flowed down her collar. A sharp pain pierced below her jaw, and she could feel her defiance and courage wilting.

"You're a foolish woman." His breath was warm against her ear. "But I am pleased to see that you are quite resourceful, for the time might come when we require your help. But remember this, and remember it well. If you refuse to comply with any of our requests, you will end up dead, like the security guard on the lobby floor."

Abby squeezed her eyes closed. Her body felt taut, as if all of her muscles were being stretched ridged. A second ticked by, and then she felt a cool shaft of air against her neck as the blade was pulled away. She relaxed her muscles and opened her eyes. Her tormentor had sauntered back toward the doorway and was squatting down to pick up what looked like a pair of old boots. The woman—Martina—stumbled in behind him, helping to haul Cal into the room.

The two robbers dropped Cal's body next to the table.

Black T-shirt bent to brush off his jeans as Martina glanced around the room, her eyes fixing on the tray in the corner. "She hit you hard, Max."

"Not so hard." The man in the black T-shirt—Max—reached up and touched a spot on his head. He looked down at his hand. "There is no blood, see? Come. Let's go. We have more important things to do at the moment than waste our time with hostages."

As the door clicked shut, Abby rushed across the room and knelt beside Cal. His eyes were closed, and at first glance, she couldn't tell whether he was alive or dead. She placed her fingers into the groove of his wrist to check his pulse, her own heart beating double time in her chest.

It felt like he had been transported from a bad dream into a painful nightmare. Cal didn't know where he was, but it sure wasn't comfortable. The surface beneath him was hard and cold. His brain felt thick and fuzzy. And he couldn't even begin to describe the agony emanating from the back of his head.

He looked up and blinked. Possibly his eyes were playing tricks on him, but the woman bent over him looked a lot like Abby Marshall. A veil of thick black hair covered most of her face, but he'd recognize that determined expression anywhere. And then he remembered. He was at the bank. Abby had gone to his truck to call for help. But instead she had been captured and dragged into the middle of the gunfight.

"Cal?" Abby's gentle voice brought him back to reality. "Are you okay?"

For a moment, he thought he saw tears in her eyes. Unlikely. Abby was as tough as they came. This was the woman who had stitched up Jake Radley after his wood-chopping accident. Who had cauterized Mayor Hovland's thumb after removing the ice pick. No, there would be no signs of sentimentality from Abby Marshall. She was far too professional for that.

He stared at her. The freckles sprinkled across her nose stood out more than usual, and her eyes were softened with concern.

And there was a trail of blood on her neck and a large, red imprint above her jaw.

"What happened to your face?"

She reached up to touch her swollen cheek and flinched as if surprised by the tenderness. "The robber named Max retaliated when I hit him with a tray. I thought that if I knocked him out, I could run through the door and escape. It's no big deal. I can't even feel it."

No big deal? Facing down an armed opponent twice her size? That sounded like a pretty big deal to him.

As Abby knelt by his side, every fiber of her being seemed to radiate confidence and control. "Hold still for a minute while I examine the cut on the back of your head."

"I'm fine," he said. But as he pushed himself up, the floor seemed to move beneath him as a wave of nausea ricocheted up his spine. He closed his eyes to regain control and then opened them up and looked around. "So we're in the break room."

Abby nodded. "Isobel Carrolls is in here with us, too. As far as I can tell, she's the only other hostage. But she seems to be in the early stages of labor."

Cal blew out a long sigh. The situation had just gone from bad to worse. He turned and quickly surveyed the room. No windows. One door. There would be no easy paths of escape.

"I'm guessing that the woman who hauled you into the lobby stopped you before you could call for backup."

Abby nodded.

"Abby?" Isobel sat up on the couch and looked around the room. "I heard you talking. Is there some- one else in the room with us? I'm having another pain now. I'm really scared."

"Sheriff Stanek is here now, but don't worry. I'm going to stay right here with you until the pain passes."

Cal watched Abby as she bent over the couch, mas- saging Isobel's shoulders and hands. In the past, he and Abby had gotten along about as well as oil and vinegar, but… He scratched his chin, feeling the start of a five- o'clock shadow. It was impossible not to admire Abby's kindness and competence. Not to mention the courage she had shown in trying to escape.

He turned his attention back to Isobel. "Can you re- member any details about how the robbery went down?"

Isobel shook her head. "It's all pretty fuzzy. It was a little before four, and everyone else was gone for the day. There were only two of us left to close up. Me and Zander. Two men and a woman burst through the door with their guns drawn. Zander tried to protect me, but they shot him before he could even pull his weapon."

Cal shook his head. "What about the alarm?"

"I would have hit it, normally. But this morning, a repairman came in to upgrade the system, and he shut the whole system all down."

Hmm. That was suspicious. "Was the bank manager aware of the work order to disable the alarm?"

"I don't know. I came in late because I had a doctor's appointment, so I heard about the whole thing second-hand." A shadow of panic crossed her eyes. "Do you think the repairman was one of the robbers?"

It made sense that someone would need to recon the space and take out the alarm ahead of the robbery. "What reason did the manager give for leaving early?"

"She found out last week that she won a weekend getaway to Miami Beach, and she was in a hurry to catch her flight." Isobel must have clocked the look of skepticism on his face because she quickly continued. "I see where you are going with this, but Tessa would never help anyone steal from the bank. She loves her job. And she'd never put me in any danger. She didn't want to leave me alone, but I insisted. West Security stops by for a midafternoon pickup, and it usually stays quiet after that. Agghh." Isobel clutched her stomach and rolled sideways.

Abby reached over and took Isobel's hand. "It's okay, Iz."

Isobel's eyes brimmed with tears. "Abby, it hurts. Will you pray with me? I'm worried about my baby boy. I just wish I knew for sure that everything was going to be okay."

"I will. But let's talk to God together. Remember that

He said, 'Where two or three are gathered in my name, there am I among them.'"

Matthew 18, verse 20. Cal knew it well.

There was a short pause and then Abby began to pray. "Dear God. We know that You have a divine plan for all of us. Help us to place our trust in You. We need Your protection. All four of us. Isobel. Cal. Me. But most especially this little baby boy who in just a short time will be entering the world. In Jesus's name, we pray. Amen."

"Amen," Cal echoed.

He had always believed in the power of prayer. His faith had sustained him through the death of his wife, Shannon, and given him hope as he faced each new day. And they certainly needed divine help now more than ever.

Especially as he remembered the complications involved in the birth of his now-ten-year-old nephew and a last-second decision to perform a Cesarean. What if Isobel's case turned out to be similar? What if her baby was breech? He could think of way too many potential problems that could only be resolved in a hospital delivery room. He cast a glance in Abby's direction. Her eyes were smudged with fatigue, and worry lines had appeared on her forehead.

Maybe she wasn't quite as confident as she had sounded. Normally, he was aware of a civilian's sensitivities. But there was something about Abby that made him forget she was operating out of her comfort zone.

Isobel groaned again and then collapsed back onto the couch, her eyes closed and her breathing steady. As impossible as it was to believe, it looked like she was about to sneak in another catnap between labor pains. Now was their chance to make a plan.

"Are you holding up okay?" He turned toward Abby and forced a small smile.

She nodded. "I am. But we need to get her out of here and to a hospital. I don't understand it, but her labor seems to be proceeding at a fast and furious rate. I can keep her comfortable and even deliver the baby if it comes to that. But I'm worried about possible complications with the birth."

He was, too. A feeling of helplessness washed over him. He needed to do something, anything, instead of just standing around and waiting for the next shoe to fall. For a second time, he raked his eyes around the room, backtracking his gaze when he noticed a vent on the side of the wall.

But before he could investigate, shouting drifted in from the hall.

"Calm down. We need to wait."

"I say we kill them now and take our chances," a woman's voice said.

Her partner was quick to respond. "No. The female hostage is a paramedic. We should keep her alive, at least for the time being, especially given Tomas's injuries. But the cowboy is expendable and can be eliminated."

Cal sucked in a long breath and looked at Abby. She was bent over the couch, tending to Isobel, and it was hard to tell whether or not she had overheard any part of the conversation.

He hoped she hadn't. Abby needed to focus on Isobel without worrying about him. The question was how long did he have before the robbers decided to pull the trigger? One minute? Ten minutes? Would he have time to make a plan?

His eyes pivoted back to the door, and pinpricks of awareness shot up his arms as he registered that the knob was slowly turning.

Apparently, he wouldn't have the luxury to weigh the options.

The door swung open, and two of the perps stepped inside. There was no sign of the older man he had shot in the lobby, but the other two—Max and Martina— had their guns drawn, clearly intending to make good on their threat.

A wave of apprehension flooded Cal's body, and he clenched his fingers into tight fists as Max moved toward Abby. "What's all the commotion?"

Abby turned and looked him in the eye. "Our friend is in labor. She needs to be taken to the hospital and seen by a doctor immediately."

Max furrowed his brow. For a moment, it appeared that he was considering her suggestion.

That's right, Max. Go see what is happening with Isobel over there on the couch, Cal offered silent encouragement as a jolt of adrenaline surged through his veins. If Max moved just a few feet farther across the room, there was a chance of engineering an escape. The door was open, and it would only take a few seconds to reach the hall. And if he made it to the lobby, he might be able to retrieve a gun from the injured shooter, and after that… He flexed his fingers and kept his eyes glued to Max.

Like a base runner on first calculating the odds of stealing to second, he edged another step closer to the door, and then—

"Stop." Martina raised her pistol and pointed it at his chest. "One more move, and you'll be dead."

Max met his partner's eye and nodded his head. "Go ahead and kill him, Martina. It's time to put an end to this silly game."

THREE

Abby stood stock-still as fear and anxiety paralyzed her limbs. If she didn't act quickly, Cal would be dead. But what could she do? Without a weapon, she couldn't stop Martina from pulling the trigger. Except… She thought back to the conversation she had heard in the hall. Maybe she wasn't completely out of options. She pushed back her shoulders and looked past Martina toward Max. He seemed to be the one in charge. And he was definitely the less trigger-happy of the two.

"If you shoot my friend, I won't help you," she said. "I won't do anything you ask of me, and I won't patch up your injured friend."

Max bent his lips into an angry sneer. "Who do you think you are? Don't you know that you are the hostage here, and hostages don't make demands of their captors? Whether or not you help us is your choice. But if you refuse to cooperate, we will kill all of you, including the pregnant woman. What do you think of that?"

Abby pulled in a deep breath and held Max's stare. Her senses raced on high alert as she tried to gauge whether Max meant what he said in the hall or if he was bluffing. It was hard to tell. His eyes were hard, and his hand holding his pistol didn't waver. But his finger wasn't on the trigger. At least not yet. "What do I think?" She returned his glare with a determined one of her own. "I don't like it. But I'm a hundred percent serious about what I just said. You can threaten me all you want, but I won't cooperate if you harm my friend."

"Ha!" Max spit out the word like a bad seed. "You think you can bargain to save your worthless companion's life. Well, you are wrong."

Dread snaked up Abby's spine. Max was calling her out. If she was going to take a stance, it was now or never. She lifted her foot to plant herself between Cal and the robbers, but before she could take a single stride, Max's lips turned up in a cruel smile as his finger closed around the trigger.

Pop! Pop! Pop!

The pistol fired three times.

Isobel's scream pierced the air as the bullets whizzed rapid-fire in quick succession, splintering through the drywall, inches from Cal's head.

Thank you, God. Abby's fingers shook as she bent over and squeezed Isobel's hand. "Stay calm, Iz. He missed. Cal's okay."

"Shut up," Max replied. "I didn't miss. I aimed at the wall on purpose. You don't know who you are dealing with here. If there are any further problems, we will shoot all three of you without a second thought. Come, Martina. Stop glaring at the cowboy. You can kill him later. We need to go and check on Tomas."

Max turned and followed Martina out of the room.

As the lock clicked in place on the door, Abby's eyes darted toward Cal, who was still standing motionless in the middle of the room. His face was a mask of controlled emotion, which made it impossible to tell what he was thinking. But how could he not be shaken and afraid? Had he thought it was the end? She had. The impossibility of the situation suddenly hit her hard. They were hostages in a bank heist with a pair of ruthless robbers who had already killed once. Was it a just a matter of time before Martina got her way and eliminated all three of them?

"Cal." Her voice shook as she met and held his glance. "I thought you were dead," she finally choked out. The rest of her words dissolved in a flood of tears.

He reached toward her and touched her arm. "Don't cry, Abby. You did good. It was incredibly courageous the way you stood your ground in the face of their threats. You didn't back down. You were tough, and they saw that. You saved my life."

"But I—" She was suddenly speechless. What Cal had just said might have been one of the nicest things anyone had ever said to her.

Isobel sat up on the couch, fear darkening her countenance. "Why are they doing this? Scaring us with bullets and threats. Why don't they just take what they came for and let us go?"

"I don't know, Iz," Abby said. Once again, she looked at Cal. His eyes held hers as he shook his head. None of this made sense. But at least for the moment, they were all still alive.

"Oh. Aggh." Isobel turned on her side and grasped her stomach. "It's happening again. Abby, help me. It hurts."

Abby swiveled around to look at the clock on the wall, silently computing the time in her head. Isobel's contractions were less than five minutes apart. Which meant that her labor continued to progress at an accelerated rate.

"Okay, Iz. I'm going to count to ten, and I want you to take small breaths and follow along with me. Ready? It's just like you learned in Lamaze class. You took Lamaze, right?"

Isobel nodded.

"Good. Concentrate on working through the pain, not fighting against it. One, two, three," Abby counted, as Isobel made an effort to control her breathing.

Abby's stomach clenched with trepidation. Isobel's pains were getting stronger—and closer together. If her calculations were correct, the baby would be born within the hour. And it would be up to her to make sure that mom and baby were both okay.

She struggled to calm her racing heart. Cal said she was brave. But she wasn't entirely sure that she was up to the challenge of delivering a baby in the break room without any of the proper supplies. The last time she helped a pregnant woman give birth, the mother-to-be was in the back seat of a Volvo, parked in front of a Dollar Store. Compared to those cramped conditions, the situation in the break room was almost luxurious. But what they gained in roominess was lost when factoring in the lack of sterile gauze, clamps or a bulb syringe. For this delivery, none of those items were available. But so far, Isobel was holding her own, though at the moment her face was pink and overheated. Of course, her blood pressure could spike at any moment. The baby could turn. Who knew what difficulties lay ahead of them?

And even if the birth took place without complications, the baby would simply become the littlest hostage.

"You doing okay, you two?" Cal moved across the room and began opening and closing the cabinets next to the sink.

"We're doing great. Isobel's a champ."

Cal stood still for a moment and then took a deep breath as if to shake off the panic of the past few minutes. He nodded and then reached up and pulled a mesh bag of oranges from a shelf above the counter. "Hey, look at this. Not the most balanced meal, but they'll do for our supper."

"Supper?" She supposed she ought to be hungry since it was well past the dinner hour. But eating was the last thing on her mind, especially after Cal's near-death encounter with Max and Martina.

Cal selected an orange from the bag and tossed it in the air. "These remind me of last June when I went deep-sea fishing in the Keys. It was a trip of a lifetime. I could have stayed there forever. Clear skies. Perfect weather. Water that sparkled in the sun."

Huh? Cal's trip to Florida last summer was an odd subject to be discussing under the circumstances. But he seemed so pleased with himself that it was easier to roll with it. Maybe he was just trying to ease the tension that lingered in the air.

"Yeah. I remember when you took that trip. Sounds like it was quite a vacation."

"Absolutely. Trolling off the coast for bluefins. Eating conch. Running my toes through the sand. On the way home, I even made a stop at Cape Canaveral. It was a spur-of-the-moment decision, but I was glad I did it. I've always been fascinated by the space program, especially the stories of the early flights. Alan Shepard. Scott Carpenter. John Glenn. Want one?" He peeled the orange and sectioned it into pieces and then held out a slice.

She shook her head, biting at a fingernail. It was an old, bad habit. Something she hadn't done in years. But the lighthearted tone of Cal's story was confusing, and she didn't cope well with situations she didn't understand.

"So, what do you know about John Glenn?" Cal asked, his eyes suddenly serious. "Apart from the fact that he was an astronaut and a senator. Did you know that when Glenn was seventy-seven, he volunteered to go back into space for one last mission? And here's a surprising fact few people recall. In 1962, he testified before a House subcommittee in favor of excluding women from the space program. After that, not one woman flew for NASA until Sally Ride."

Aha. Her lips tightened. Cal had always been supportive of females in the department, so she wasn't sure where his story was going. But she was prepared for an unexpected twist in the tale.

He popped two sections of the orange in his mouth and chewed them thoughtfully. He waited as she helped

Isobel through another hard contraction and then he continued. "Of course, Glenn changed his mind and went on to support the careers of a number of women in the program. He showed the world how he learned from his mistake and how he was determined to make amends."

"Uh-huh." From the knowing pleat at the corner of his mouth, it was clear that there was going to be an additional punch line to hammer home the moral of the story just to be sure.

"The important part of the learning curve is what comes afterward." He dropped his gaze to meet hers. "The unexpected opportunity to reset the scene and start again. Like with the two of us."

Well, she hadn't seen that coming. A flush of heat crept up her neck. Was Cal referring to the awkward vibe that had existed between the two of them since their disastrous attempt at a first date? The story about John Glenn was certainly a roundabout method of opening the discussion, but she appreciated the effort.

Because the way it had all gone down bothered her, as well. She certainly hadn't handled the situation with finesse or grace at any point in its unfolding. It had taken months dodging matchmaking attempts by mutual friends before she had reluctantly agreed to meet Cal for dinner.

Their so-called date happened a year-and-a-half ago, but her cheeks still burned at the memory of how she had left Cal waiting at the restaurant when she called at the last minute to cancel. She hadn't even offered a credible excuse. It was bad form on her part, but here was Cal, suggesting that they ought to "reset the scene and start again."

If it was only that easy.

She pulled in a deep breath and let it out slowly. This was her opportunity to explain her reasons for bailing on him that night. But that would mean telling Cal about the adoption.

"I'm sorry that I didn't show up that night for our dinner. The truth is, I was about to leave for the restaurant when I got a call from Children and Family Services about Davey Lightfoot."

"Davey Lightfoot?" Cal's eyebrows shot up. "I know him. Tough family situation. Great kid, though."

"I agree." Abby beamed. "And—" She hesitated. But she had gone this far, so she might as well present Cal with the whole unvarnished truth. "I had just begun the process of trying to adopt him, and I was hitting all the usual roadblocks along the way. As you know, his Mom passed away about two years ago, and his father died in a boating accident before he was born. His grandparents knew they couldn't handle raising a small child on their own, but they weren't certain if foster care was a better solution. For a while, it looked like the adoption wasn't going to happen at all. The night of our date, I got a call that they wanted to meet with me and Davey's social worker to talk about the next step in moving the process forward. I had to go. I couldn't say no, but I should have explained what was going on."

"So?" He raised an interested brow. "It's been over a year. Has the adoption been approved?"

She shrugged. "Maybe. That call I missed when I

dropped my phone outside on the stoop might have provided an answer to that question. I can only hope and pray that it was good news and when and if we get out of here, I can start making plans to bring Davey home."

"I hope so, too." Cal's grin was wide and warm. Really, his face was transformed when he smiled. His eyes crinkled at the edges, and his features softened just enough to hide the gruffness of his outward demeanor. "I'm glad you told me, Abby. It's not something I generally talk about, but I'm adopted, too. And I was blessed to be raised by two of the most wonderful parents in the world. So I really admire what you're trying to do for Davey. And to your other point, I assure you that we are getting out of here, so you need to start organizing your to-do list to get ready to bring Davey home to live with you."

She smiled back at him. It was kind of Cal to focus on the positive and not remind her—at least not directly—that she was mostly to blame for the awkwardness between them. Kind. That was what he was. But just because Cal was being cordial didn't change the fact that their date had been a mistake. Neither one of them had been looking for a relationship. She had only agreed to meet him for dinner as a way of silencing the matchmakers. Romance had never been part of her long-term plan. Besides, she was all in on adopting Davey. And Cal still seemed the same grieving widower he had been when he arrived in town. He never spoke of his late wife, but his silence suggested a deep pain.

"I really appreciate the support, Cal. And I'm glad for the chance to clear the air by telling you about Davey."

There was a sound of shuffling from the couch, and Abby turned her attention back to her patient. Isobel's eyes blinked open as she turned and faced Abby. "Do you really think I am going to have my baby tonight?"

"Maybe. But right now, you have to listen to your body and stay as relaxed as you can."

"I'll try. I just wish I could be more like you. You always seem so calm."

"That's kind of you to say, Iz. But it has taken years of practice. I almost fainted the first time I had to give CPR. And growing up, I hated the sight of blood."

"Seriously? How did you end up becoming a paramedic?"

The event that dictated the future course of her life flashed before her eyes. The shattered glass. The scent of burning rubber. The wail of sirens. The trail of blood. She shook off the memory. She still thought about her father's death almost every day, but she hadn't talked about it in years. Hadn't dreamt about it for even longer than that.

"It's a long story. Maybe we can talk about it later."

"Okay." Isobel winced as another contraction pulled her into its grip. "Help me, please. I feel like my insides are being squeezed by an iron grip."

Abby shifted into high gear. "Try not to fight it. Roll with the pain. You have to let the contractions do their job."

"I'm trying. But it's hard."

Abby reached over and took Isobel's hand. "You're doing great. But remember, these things come in waves.

Once one crests, you need to start preparing for the next one, okay?"

Isobel nodded.

"Is there anything we can do to make her more comfortable?" Cal asked.

Abby shook her head. "Not at the moment."

"Okay, then. If you don't need me, I'm going to check out that vent on the wall. There's something not quite right about this whole setup. The robbers sure seem to be taking their time clearing the money out of the vault. I'm going to try to crawl through to the room next door and see if I can find out anything about their plan. Better yet, I might find a way for us to get out of here before Max and Martina come back."

"That would be great, Cal," she said distractedly. "Isobel seems to be entering the transitional stage of her labor. It won't be long before she needs to push." She met Cal's eye, silently transmitting a somber message: the baby might well be born in the break room of the bank, whether any of them liked it or not.

Cal crouched down on the floor and began loosening the screws on the wall vent. "Just tug on my feet if you need me," he called over to Abby.

"Sounds good," Abby said. She seemed so focused on helping Isobel through her next contraction that he could have told her he was heading to Starbucks for coffee and she probably wouldn't have noticed or cared.

Using a short Phillips-head screwdriver he had found in a drawer, he removed the four screws holding the vent cover in place. Once the last one was loosened, he set the metal piece onto the floor and tried to estimate the size of the opening. Three feet by two feet? Maybe a bit larger. It wasn't huge, but there was room enough for him to slither through if he pressed his stomach flat against the bottom and tried not to think about being squashed like a pancake. Dust swirled through the air as he inched forward, a shaft of light guiding him toward the opening on the opposite wall.

He flexed his shoulders to keep them from cramping up and let his mind drift back to his first few weeks on the job as sheriff of Dagger Lake. He had barely finished arranging his desk when the mayor's secretary stuck her head into his office to tell him about Abby. "Cute, sweet and perfect in all ways." That had been the first effort in what turned out to be a determined campaign to set the two of them up. And there were certain third parties—Abby's brother, for one—who hadn't been willing to take no for an answer.

After months of resisting, he had finally given in and asked Abby out to dinner. But when she didn't show up, he was glad. As lovely as Abby was, he wasn't ready to embark on a new relationship, especially not with someone who reminded him so much of his ex-wife. His marriage had not been a particularly successful one, but the last few years had been especially rough. He had taken it hard when Shannon was killed, and, even now, three years after the shooting, he was still untangling all the complicated emotions swirling in his mind.

The vent narrowed slightly as he edged the last few inches toward the opening. The slats on the wall were partially open, and he used his fingers to pry them up the rest of the way.

It was hard to tell from his reduced perspective, but the room seemed to have the same basic layout, beige carpet and white walls as the break room. His breath caught in his throat as he looked down, and a tingle of alarm wound down his spine. This wasn't good. Stacks of cellophane-wrapped packages were spread across the floor. He recognized their putty-like shape as well as the faint aroma of tar. C-4. A plastic explosive. That was powerful stuff. And there was a lot of it. Way more than it would take to blow up a safe. It was all over the room, not just around the vault. He leaned in closer for a better view.

As his brain registered what his eyes were seeing, his pulse began pounding in his head. Dread washed across his senses as he realized that everything he thought he knew about the robbery was incorrect. He had assumed that Max, Martina and Tomas were a trio of robbers intent on breaking into the vault. That was wrong. He'd reckoned that when push came to shove, it would be two against one. Even that was wrong.

A new set of feet stood in that far corner of the room. A pair of brown wing-tip shoes. A fourth criminal.

But judging by his imperious tone, he was the one calling the shots.

And even worse.

At the man's feet was a car seat. Just the right size for an infant. And next to the base was a stack of baby clothes and a package of diapers.

It was so much more sinister than he had imagined.

This wasn't a bank robbery. It was a kidnapping.

And there was enough C-4 in the room to blow up the entire building.

He took a deep breath. It would take time to process this new information. But his brain flashed into overdrive as he struggled to make sense of it all. There had been countless indications that this was more than a run-of-the-mill robbery. Realization dawned. Maybe the injured robber had medical training. Which, in turn, explained why Abby was still alive. With Tomas out of commission, they needed to keep a paramedic at the ready.

At least until the baby was born.

And just like that, his optimism evaporated. There was a cruel tone to the new man's voice, a calculating edge that spoke of a cold-blooded killer.

A killer who would blow up the bank with all the hostages inside. And with the amount of C-4 the robbers had stockpiled, any evidence would be incinerated.

But who would risk so much to kidnap a baby? Sure, there were plenty of people out there who wanted children. But what kind of person would commit a crime of this complexity to abduct a newborn? The scheme was more elaborate than anything he had come across in all his years of police work. The bank's isolated location made it the perfect place to stage a kidnapping, with the added bonus of confiscating the cash on hand. The person behind such a devious plan had to be a relative or family member. It was the only thing that made any sense.

He scooted a few inches forward, hoping to glean

something from the men's conversation that would help him understand the nature of their plan.

The blaring jingle of a cell phone set his heart racing. Leaning in, he heard the new man answer. "Ricky."

Now he had a name.

Slowly and carefully, he pushed away from the grate. He needed to get back to the room to talk to Isobel. To find out who Ricky was. To ask Abby to slow down the labor. Because, if he was right, the moment Isobel's son entered the world, the kidnappers would snatch him from his mother's arms and blow up the building with the hostages inside.

But as he shoved his arms forward to propel himself back, his pant pocket snagged on the seam of the vent. He jiggled his body to release the catch. Sweat beaded on his brow as the metal casing gave an ominous creak. Within the narrow confines of the vent, the noise echoed with a deafening groan. His heart jackknifed in his chest. Had the men in the other room heard? Should he continue to shift backward in case they barged into the break room to investigate? No. He could just make out the muffled sounds of hushed conversation.

"It came from over here." The voice sounded like Max.

His body froze. Had they found him? Had he just jeopardized Abby and Isobel through his careless haste? A cold band of unease wrapped around his body. He closed his eyes and then opened them to peer through the slats. A pair of black Converse sneakers blocked his view.

"Probably just a rat in the air ducts." Martina's strident voice carried clear. "This building is so decrepit we're doing it a favor by blowing it up."

He held his breath. A few seconds later, Max walked away from the vent. That was way too close. And they were very nearly out of time. He needed to talk to Abby now. With sweaty palms, he resumed his exit. With a few backward thrusts, he slid out of the vent. His heart was racing, but he smoothed his face into a bland expression as he walked across the room. He needed answers, but not at the risk of causing Isobel any unnecessary distress. She would have to be told the truth eventually, but not yet.

He waited until Isobel relaxed from her latest contraction before stepping closer to the couch. "How are you doing?" he asked.

"Pretty good." Isobel's smile was strained.

"Quick random question. Is the baby's dad in the picture, or are you planning to raise your son on your own?"

Abby shot him a look. "Maybe now's not the best time for this kind of conversation."

"No. It's okay, Abby." Isobel's upper lip trembled. "My husband doesn't know about the baby, Cal. I ran away when I found out that I was pregnant." A large teardrop ran down her face. "It's not a story with a happy ending."

A protective surge rushed through his gut. He had seen that same terror-filled expression too many times in his line of work. It was worn by women who had suffered abuse and live in fear for their lives. Like so many others, Isobel had been hurt in the past, her present was dismal and her future looked fatal. He reached across the sofa and took hold of her hand. "I understand. I won't ask any more questions. But can you at least tell me your husband's name?" He held his breath, though he knew the answer before she replied.

"Ricky," she whispered through a veil of tears.

FOUR

Cal's eyes had that hundred-mile look of a man who had no idea what to do next. Clearly, he had seen something in the room next door and, judging by the shadow darkening his countenance, it wasn't good.

What had he witnessed or heard that was making him so agitated? Abby wasn't sure that she wanted to know. She closed her eyes to gather her thoughts. When she opened them, Cal was standing next to her with his back to the couch.

"We have a problem," he whispered.

"What?" she breathed back.

He took a step away from the sofa and beckoned her to follow. "I saw someone new in the room next door, and there's a good chance it was Isobel's husband, Ricky. Is there anything you can do to delay the baby's birth?"

She shook her head. "At this point, that would be impossible. What's going on?"

A muscle tensed in Cal's jaw. "It's starting to look as if Isobel's husband is the mastermind of this whole scheme. I don't know how long he's been here at the bank. But he has a car seat and some clothes and diapers, so it's safe to assume that he's aiming to leave with more than just cash. I suspect he's planning to make a grab for the kid."

"What about Isobel? Do you think he wants to abduct her, as well?"

"What are you two talking about?" Isobel's anxious voice interrupted their hushed conversation. "Is everything all right? Is something wrong with the baby?"

Abby's brain froze, and she was unable to choke out even a straightforward reply. "Your little boy is fine, Iz. Just give me a minute to talk to Cal." She turned and followed Cal to the corner of the room.

He leaned his head close to hers, unease coursing across his countenance. "How long do we have until the baby is born? Twenty minutes? A half hour?"

"It could be as long as that, but it's hard to say."

"Okay. But as soon as Isobel gives birth, we're going to need to get out of here fast. Right now, Max and Martina are laying explosives to blow up the bank. We need to stop them. But at this point, I'm out of ideas."

She fought against the hopelessness threatening to overtake her. "We'll think of something, Cal. We've got to save Isobel and the baby." But when she turned her head, her heart jumped in her chest. A moment earlier, her patient had been fine. But now she appeared to be in the throes of a full-on panic attack. Her eyes were huge against her face, and her breathing was quick and shallow.

"I can't do this, Abby. I thought that I was ready, but I'm not. I can't have my baby in a bank. It's not sanitary.

What if he gets a disease? What if he catches a cold? I have the cutest little outfit packed in my overnight bag for him. A set of footie pajamas with a pointy, striped hood in supersoft cotton that won't irritate his skin. I was going to bring it to the hospital for him to wear home. But now I don't have anything. He'll be naked and shivering, and I don't even have a diaper or an undershirt to keep him warm."

She could understand what Isobel was feeling. It was natural to focus on the minor details even as the world seemed to be falling apart.

"It's going to be okay, Iz. Babies are born every day under less-than-perfect conditions. Just think of the story your little guy will be able to tell the other kids when he gets older. That he was born in a bank, during a robbery, and that his mom was courageous and brave."

"I don't know Abby. I don't feel courageous or brave. I feel scared."

"We're all scared, Iz. But we have to have faith. Hasn't God taken care of us so far?"

Isobel sniffled and then nodded her head. "He has. And I'm grateful I don't have to go through this alone. I couldn't ask for a better support team than you and Cal. But everything is happening so fast that I can't even process it. What am I going to wrap the baby in once he's born? He'll be so tiny and cold."

Abby had been thinking the same thing. Both the infant and Isobel would require extra warmth after the trauma of birth. She looked at Cal. He was obviously agitated, as evidenced by his relentless pacing across the floor. She could feel his adrenaline mixing with her own rising panic.

And then she remembered something she had noticed while she first looked around the room. In one of the drawers next to the sink were oversize dish towels, the right size for swaddling a newborn. They weren't perfect, but they'd do in a pinch.

"Hey, Cal," she called out. "Would you mind grabbing a few of those dish towels in the drawer?"

"On it." Cal was halfway across the room when Isobel's voice stopped him in his tracks.

"Wait. I know!" She pointed toward the ceiling. "There are a bunch of blankets upstairs in the attic."

Cal turned his head, his eyes burning with excitement. "This place has an attic?"

Abby looked up, a gasp catching in her throat. There it was, plain as day when you knew what to look for— a wooden panel set flush with the tiles that offered access to the attic above.

She held her breath as Cal pulled a chair across the room, climbed up on the seat and yanked hard on the latch. Nothing happened. His jaw tightened as he pulled harder. With a slow creak, the panel opened to reveal a set of collapsible stairs. He gave another hard tug, and a hinged staircase unfolded to the floor.

"Piece of cake." Cal climbed down from his perch and set his foot on the bottom step of the staircase. "I'll get those blankets and see what else I can find up there. If anyone comes to the door, you'll have to stall them until I can maneuver this contraption back in place."

"Sure thing." Abby still couldn't believe her eyes.

But there was no denying the sight of Cal's boots disappearing into the square opening at the top of the stairs.

"Abby?" Isobel pulled herself up to a sitting position, a frantic look on her face. "I think I need to push."

Abby scooted next to Isobel and reached for her hand. "Okay, Iz. This is the moment we've been waiting for. Keep your chin tucked in and just bear down when you feel the pressure. I'll be here with you, helping you all the way. Are you ready to give it a go?"

Isobel nodded. "Ready as I'll ever be."

"Good." Abby waited until the contraction began to subside. "Good job. But you need to rest now so you'll be ready when the next one rolls around. And remember that the important thing is not to fight the pain."

Silence settled over the room, punctured only by Isobel's breathing. Isobel's gaze searched to meet hers. "Is it okay if we talk a little bit more? I was hoping we could discuss something that relates to what Cal asked about my husband. I told Cal that Ricky didn't know about the baby, and that's true. But I didn't mention that the baby was the reason I ran away. I had been planning to leave for a long time, but finding out that I was pregnant sealed the deal."

"You were afraid that he would be angry when he heard your news?" Abby guessed.

"Actually, it was the opposite. I knew that once he found out he'd never let me go."

"How could he stop you?"

"That's the part I didn't want to tell Cal. With him being the sheriff and all, I was afraid I'd be judged by association. Ricky pretends to be a regular guy and a hardworking businessman, but none of that's true. He operates outside of the law, dealing drugs and engaging in human trafficking. He's been caught a couple of times, but his attorneys always get him off on some technicality. He'd never rest if he thought I was keeping him away from his only son."

"Cal wouldn't judge you if he knew the truth. He wouldn't think less of you because you made a mistake and married the wrong man."

Isobel fiddled with a loose piece of her hair. "Maybe not. But there's another reason why I want to keep my past a secret. I can't tell Cal about Ricky because I don't want him thinking this is a problem he can solve. Because it isn't. No one can take Ricky down. *No one.* Anyone who tries ends up dead."

Isobel's face contorted in pain as the next contraction took hold. Talking about her husband was clearly adding to her distress, but she returned to the subject the moment the discomfort subsided. "It's true, Abby. Ricky hurts everyone who crosses him. In his world, there are no second chances. Revenge and avenge. That's the creed he lives by, with no exceptions."

"As far as you know, he is unaware of your pregnancy?"

A shadow passed across Isobel's face. "If Ricky knew about the baby, I wouldn't be here. He'd pull out all stops to track me down. If he found out I was pregnant when I left, he'd kill me."

"He'd *kill* you?" The man Isobel was describing sounded like a monster. A monster who was right next door. A cold chill of dread washed over her as the likelihood of any of them surviving until morning began to seem more and more remote.

Isobel must have noted her distress because she reached over and squeezed Abby's hand. "Don't worry about Ricky. He has no way of knowing where I am."

If only that were true.

A creak in the hallway caused Abby's eyes to dart toward the exposed staircase. Did she have time to push it back in place? Isobel's murmurings sounded dim and faraway as she rushed across the room and clutched the sides of the folding steps. Gripping the slats with clenched fingers, she pushed hard, but the mechanism moved only a few inches before snapping back to the floor. All that was left to do was block the door and employ her persuasive skills to keep the intruders at bay. She clenched her fingers into fists as she waited for the click of a key in the lock.

A minute passed. Then another. It appeared they were safe, at least for the moment, although it was only a matter of time before one of the criminals returned to the room.

Of course, Isobel was unaware of the specifics of the latest threat, and Abby planned to keep her in the dark for as long as possible. Fear could cause Isobel's body to shut down and trigger complications for her unborn child. No matter what might happen later, Abby's only goal at the moment was to ensure a safe delivery of Isobel's little boy.

As Isobel worked through her next contraction, Abby laid out her meager supplies. Two bottles of water. A bowl. A towel. And a roll of dental floss to tie off the umbilical cord. Given Cal's recent discovery about the robbers' real intentions, it was likely that somewhere, probably in the room next door, there was a cache of provisions that had been brought along for the delivery. Like a bulb syringe that would allow her to suction the mucus from the newborn's nose and mouth. And a vitamin K shot. And erythromycin eye ointment for the baby's eyes.

But there was no point in fretting about things she couldn't control. Better to concentrate on doing what she could to ensure a safe delivery. She drummed her fingers against the side of the couch, trying to anticipate every possible complication.

Isobel shot her a questioning glance. "Is there something going on that I don't know about? Because Cal seemed pretty frantic before he left."

It was time for some diplomatic backpedaling. "Cal has been working hard to find a way to get us out of here. But once the baby is born, we may need to move fast."

Isobel nodded, her eyes shining with resolve. "You can count on me."

It was impossible not to be impressed by her courage. She had run away from an abusive relationship, moved to a place she had never been before, gotten a job and now she was about to give birth in the break room of a bank. "You're an incredible woman, Iz. You've shown an amazing amount of courage in the way you've stayed so positive through this ordeal."

Isobel shook her head. "The thing is, Abby, I'm not usually very brave. I think that's why I ended up married to Ricky. When I met him, he was extremely charming. He kept asking me out until I finally gave in. His persistence was a definite boost to my ego. And he knew how to pull out all the stops to make a good impression."

Abby was preparing a follow-up question when a booted foot appeared on the top rung of the staircase.

Cal made his way down to the break room. She couldn't see his face, so there was no way to know if he had found anything useful in the attic, but her heart beat faster at each measured step. When he reached the bottom and turned his head, she slowly expelled the air in her chest. He was smiling. That crooked smile of his that crinkled his eyes and hinted that momentum finally had turned their way.

"I've got blankets for the baby," he said, setting a pile of fleece throws onto the floor. There was an edge of excitement in his voice. Clearly, he had discovered something more significant. "I only grabbed five, but there are more. And they were packaged in plastic, so they're clean and moth-free. I also found a pair of trainers that might be your size." He handed the shoes to Abby. She glanced over at her discarded pumps, grateful for the thoughtful gesture.

"Thanks, Cal," she said.

"You're welcome. We can't have you hobbling around in bare feet. How's our patient doing?"

"So far, so good." Abby tilted her head to the side. What was he not telling them? What else had he discovered under the rafters?

His lips bent into a pleased smile. "I couldn't find a

light switch. But there's a full moon shining through a skylight in the roof, so it was bright enough for me to spot a pile of sleds stacked on the floor."

"Oh. Right. They were left over from a promotion we did last Thanksgiving," Isobel explained. "We gave away about five dozen, but Tessa saved the rest. She never throws anything away."

"Well, I for one am glad she's a pack rat," Cal said. "Because they just might be the key to our escape. I still have a few things to figure out, so I'm going back up to see if there's something I missed. Same strategy as before if anyone comes to the door."

Cal's excitement was palpable. But what was the plan? "We don't have much time," Abby said. "Isobel's getting close to delivering the baby. It could happen any minute."

He turned to look at Isobel. "Hang in there, kid. Abby's great at this stuff, so you couldn't be in better hands." And with that, he began to climb up the stairs.

Cal had made it halfway across the attic when he stopped and looked down at the floor. If his estimation was correct, the kidnappers were gathered directly below the spot where he was standing. At this point, they were probably getting anxious, waiting for the baby to be born. For Max and Martina, there was money on the line. They were hired guns, probably looking for a payout of cash from the robbery. He had dealt with criminals like them before. When caught, they were quick to lawyer up, always with one eye on the possibility of a plea bargain. But their leader was a different story. Ricky would be a formidable foe, quick to turn even a small mistake to an immediate advantage.

But at this point, none of them knew about the attic. And Cal aimed to keep it that way by treading as silently as possible over the creaking wooden boards.

First up—the sleds. The cheap plastic shell would offer little protection against a rough terrain, and the flimsy handles looked like they could break with one hard pull. On the positive side, they would be light enough to skim across the deep drifts of snow.

Second item on the agenda—the skylight, which was cut in to a section of the roof almost level with the floor. Another positive. So was the fact that the mechanism itself was an older model with a spring-loaded screen on the front designed to provide ventilation. He knelt down and spun the crank. It was just as he hoped. The opening was wide enough to fit a sled.

He pushed out the screen and watched it slide sideways across the shingles. The slope was steep, and the snow was still coming down. But the roof itself extended all the way to the ground where a deep drift would soften their landing.

It wasn't a perfect escape plan, but at this point, it was their only option.

He headed over to a bin at the far end of the attic and retrieved the wooden shims that he had spotted on his last visit. Thanks again to Tessa and her unwillingness to throw things away, he would have plenty of wedges to jam under the break room door. Then he placed his left foot on the top step of the staircase and headed down to the break room.

His feet had barely hit the ground when he heard the bleating of a newborn's first cry. Isobel's baby had been born.

He hurried toward the couch and looked down at the infant curled on his mother's chest. His body was red and wrinkled, and his arms and legs seemed too long for his pint-size frame. There were a few tufts of dark brown hair on his otherwise bald head, and a pair of bright pink lips framed his rosebud mouth. In other words, he was perfect.

"Nicely done, Iz," he said.

"Abby deserves all of the credit." Isobel's voice was woozy with relief. "I could never have done it without her."

He looked at Abby. She was smiling as she wiped away a tear. Admiration and a pang of something deeper—something he hadn't felt in a very long time—exploded in his chest.

"Want to hold him for a minute while I take care of mom?" Abby said.

He nodded.

Abby picked up the baby and, with the edge of a towel, gently wiped off the little boy's head. She swaddled him in one of the blankets, tucking in the sides to form a tight pouch. Then she set the blue bundle in his arms.

He had held babies before. Three of his sisters had kids, and he had visited the hospital when they were born. But there was something extraordinary about a birth under such difficult circumstances, and it was hard not to be overcome with the wonder of it.

"Does he have a name?"

Isobel shook her head as the thud of footsteps pounded in the hall. Ricky and his henchmen had come to claim their prize. There was no time to delay. Defend and protect. It was the only way. Nothing was going to happen to Isobel and Abby and the little boy nestled in his arms, not if he had anything to say about it. He handed the infant back to Isobel and picked up the stapler. It wasn't much of a weapon, but the element of surprise would be on his side, at least for the first few seconds.

Abby touched his shoulder, lowering her voice as she pointed toward the door. "I have an idea. Let me see if I can stall them, at least for a few minutes."

He nodded. It was worth a try. A key turned in the lock. It was the moment of reckoning.

Abby waited in front of the door. With the stapler gripped in his right hand, Cal pressed his back against the wall where he could remain invisible to the robbers. The knob turned, and Abby poked her head through the ten-inch opening. "Hey, hi, there, Max, Martina, and… who are you again?"

Ricky? Cal guessed, but he couldn't be sure.

"We heard noises. Has the baby been born?" Max's tone was hushed and soothing, but there was an impatient edge to his question.

Abby compressed her body further into the crack. "Yes, Max. Isobel just gave birth to a little boy. She's fine, and the baby appears to be healthy, as well. But I need to do an assessment one minute after delivery, and then five minutes later to verify the results. Basically, it's an evaluation of the infant's color, heart rate, muscle tone and respiratory effort. After the second check, I'll assign an Apgar score, which is normally somewhere between five and ten. I've just finished the first check, and I'll do the next one in just a few minutes. So far, so good, I'm happy to report. It certainly looks like Isobel has been blessed with a healthy little son. Which reminds me, I ought to get back and assist with the afterbirth. Before I go, is there something I can do for you?"

"We demand to see the baby."

Cal flinched. That was definitely Ricky's voice issuing orders. He shifted his eyes to Isobel. A look of absolute terror consumed her countenance as she clutched her tiny son tightly in her arms. Her eyes met his and appealed for help. He raised his chin, signaling the need for patience. So far, Abby was more than holding her own and managing to avoid a violent confrontation.

"That's fine. I understand." Abby kept her tone light, allowing that it was the most natural thing in the world for three armed bank robbers to concern themselves with a stranger's newborn. "I will have the baby cleaned up and ready for you to see if you will just permit me ten minutes to finish the assessment."

"You can have five minutes," Ricky spit out. "And not a second longer."

As the lock clicked into place, Cal went into overdrive. Abby had bought them five minutes. Three hundred short seconds, with the countdown beginning right now.

"Don't forget our coats. We can put them on when

we're in the attic!" he whispered to Abby as he sprinted across the room. First order of business was barricading the door. He pushed a chair under the knob and then dropped to his knees. He split open a package of shims and began wedging them in place. This was a first. He'd never blocked an entryway before, though he had busted through many as a cop.

In the background, he could hear Abby encouraging Isobel to set the baby down on the couch so she could help her slip on the large men's coat they had found stuffed in one of the cubbies.

"This isn't my jacket. It belongs to Zander." Isobel sobbed as fresh tears flowed down her cheeks. "Oh, poor Zander. What will happen to his family?"

"I know it's hard to think about that, Iz. But we just need to get moving up the steps."

"But why can't I carry my little boy with me up to the attic?" Isobel pleaded as Abby nudged her toward the stairs. "What if something happens while we're gone?"

"Cal will be here. And I'll come right back down here to get him and bring him to you. I won't leave him alone a minute longer than necessary."

"Please, Abby. That was Ricky's voice on the other side of the door. I'd know it anywhere. He has come for the baby, hasn't he? But I won't let him take him. I would rather die than let that man lay a hand on my son."

"Shh," Abby said. "Cal and I have no intention of letting your little boy out of our sight. We worked too hard to get you this far. We're not about to let some thug kidnap your son."

"Kidnap?" Isobel's voice was tinged with hysteria.

Out of the corner of his eye, Cal could see Isobel's body lurch sideways. But Abby was right behind her, poised to keep her from falling to the ground.

"Is that what all of this is about?" Isobel wanted to know. "Those men didn't come to rob the bank. They were hired by Ricky to take my baby!"

"That may have been their plan, but we are not going to let them succeed. Take one step at a time, Isobel. I'm right behind you. And Cal is ready to help, too."

"I'm right here if you need me," he chimed in from his spot by the door. He had to hand it to both women. Isobel's response to the situation was relatively measured, given the circumstances, and Abby—well, there was no other word for her short of amazing. It was astonishing how adroitly she had dealt with Ricky while he had barked his commands.

"Take it slow and easy." He heard Abby murmur as she threaded her hand around Isobel's waist and helped support her weight as they walked across the room. "I'm going to let go and you can grab hold of the ladder. I'm right behind you if you feel weak."

With a final flourish, Cal wedged the last half dozen shims into the side of the frame. They wouldn't do much to slow the men down, but even a few seconds could make a difference. Once he finished with the shims, he began adding to the barricade. Anything and everything that wasn't nailed down needed to be hauled as quietly as possible across the room and propped against the door.

Three minutes passed in the blink of an eye. The

baby started to wail just as Abby returned to the bottom of the stairs. "See you in a minute," she said. Then, she tucked the infant under the crook of her arm and headed back to the attic.

After pushing the last couple of chairs in place, he turned off the light and climbed up the stairs. When he reached the attic, he unhinged the ladder and pulled the clasp. The panel ticked into place, but a second later it clicked out. The snap wasn't holding.

Twice more, he attempted the lock.

And twice more, he failed.

FIVE

The baby's cry was so soft that it seemed laced with feathers, but it caused pangs of concern in his mother's eyes.

"Abby..." Isobel slumped against a crossbeam, barely able to stand.

"Rest for a moment, Iz, and gather your strength. As soon as you feel up to it, you can hold your little boy."

"I should have told you about the broken latch. The janitor usually closes it for us. We always..." Isobel's tears fell and stained the wooden floorboards.

Cal released the panel and pulled himself to his feet. "Don't worry about it. The barricade at the door ought to slow them down enough to give us a head start. You know that old saying, when God closes a door, He opens a window? Well, that's literally what He's done for us tonight. We've got a couple of sleds, an open skylight, a slanted roof and a soft drop to the ground. Not to mention lots of snow for a fast ride down to the road at the bottom. We might have to wait for a few minutes for someone to drive by. But when they do, we'll flag them down and call nine-one-one. Make sense?"

"Uh-huh." Abby grimaced through chattering teeth. It made sense, but it wouldn't be easy. She looked down at the baby, still nestled in her arms. He looked even smaller and frailer wrapped in his thick cocoon of blankets, his serious blue eyes staring up at her so trustingly.

A gust of wind blasted through the skylight, dusting the floorboards with a shower of downy flakes. Even in their winter coats, the attic was cold, and it would be even chillier once they got outside.

Cal walked across the attic and picked up two of the sleds. "Let me set these up for launching. Abby, you go down first with Isobel and the baby, and I'll follow behind."

"No. You're heavier, so your sled will go faster. Isobel is losing blood, and she's the one most at risk. Getting her to the hospital has to be priority one. You go first with Isobel and the baby, and I'll follow your path."

Isobel's eyes blazed with fear. "What if Ricky gets to the road ahead of us and tries to grab my little boy?"

Cal pulled in a long breath. "You can trust me, Isobel. He won't get his hands on your baby without a fight."

Isobel bent over and brushed a kiss against the baby's forehead. After a second, she raised her head, her eyes sad with resignation. Abby choked back her own tears. Isobel's terror was rooted in the knowledge of the man who had tracked her down with the goal of kidnapping his son. She knew better than any of them the lengths to which Ricky would go to ensure that his will prevailed.

Fists banged against the break room door.

Their five minutes were up. It was go time.

Abby clutched the baby to her chest to warm herself against the chill. The air escaping through the open skylight was as frigid as a hole in a frozen lake where someone might drop a line in the hope of catching a fish.

Ice fishing. Judging from Cal's attire that was what he'd been planning to do, right now, instead of helping Isobel settle into position on a plastic orange sled.

Bam! Bam! Bam! The pounding intensified, rattling the floorboards under her feet.

"Okay, Isobel," Cal said. "Let's load up you two and take a ride."

Cal seemed oddly upbeat, considering what lay ahead. He was embarking on a terrifying journey down an icy roof, through a maze of pine trees, toward the shoulder of the major road. It would only make sense for him to be worried about their chances.

He draped a blanket around Isobel's shoulders and folded a second to form a cushion at the bottom of the sled. "Don't worry. I'm an expert at steering these things. My sisters could tell you stories about how I once rode down a practice course for the luge."

Was he serious? Maybe not, but his relaxed banter had the desired effect. Isobel smiled as she scooted forward to make room for Cal on the sled. But her eyes remained uneasy and dark with distress. She had to be exhausted. Minutes after giving birth, she had climbed up a rickety staircase to the attic. But like Cal, she was pretending that setting off on a moonlight ride down a snowy embankment was fun.

Cal turned to Abby. "As soon as we clear the roof,

grab the other sled and follow us down. Though you can still change your mind and go first."

"No," she said. "I really think this is the best plan for all of us."

"Okay, then," Cal said. He reached over and touched her hand. The sensation of Cal's fingers brushing against her skin sent a rush of warmth flaring in her cheeks. Her breath caught in her throat, tangling her words into a murmur.

Cal turned to Isobel. "Abby's going to hand you the baby now, and we'll be on our way."

"No! Wait!" Isobel's eyes had a look of terror as she shook her head. "I can't do this. I don't feel strong enough to hold him. What if I pass out and drop him, and he falls into the snow? He could tumble down the hill out of our reach. And what if we aren't able to find him out there, lost and alone in the darkness?"

Time seemed to stop as the sled teetered on the precipice of the open skylight. Abby's eyes found Cal's as he shook his head. Isobel was hysterical, but there wasn't time to argue or to consider a change in the plan.

Bam! Bam! Bam! The kidnappers hammered even harder against the break room door.

Boom.

The crack of splintering wood sent vibrating waves across the attic floor.

A muscle clenched in Cal's jaw. The time for hesitation was gone. "Okay, Abby. You take the baby on the sled. We'll meet at the bottom by the road." His voice was calm, but the set of his mouth betrayed the desperation of the moment.

Abby nodded, and then Cal leaned forward and pushed off the roof.

As soon as the sled disappeared from her sight, Abby switched into high gear. She needed to find a way to protect the tiny infant while freeing her hands to steer the sled. If only she could fashion some sort of a sling which would keep Isobel's little boy close to her chest. But there was no time for that. Clutching the baby in her arms, she rushed toward the skylight and positioned the second sled on the edge. In an empty crate she found under the rafters, she made a cocoon of blankets to cushion her tiny passenger.

The tone and desperate pitch of the shouting in the room below hastened her movements. It was impossible not to think about what Isobel had said about Ricky— that he was a man who would stop at nothing to get his own way. How strange it was to think that in the six months she had known the pregnant teller, sat next to her at Bible study, chatted with her at the bank, in all that time, there hadn't been the slightest inkling of the troubles she carried in her heart.

As Abby set the crate in front of her and settled down on the back end of the sled, she pictured a time when Isobel would be able to put the darkness behind her, when she would be free to raise her little boy away from Ricky's lurking shadow and the fear of his vengeful wrath. It filled her with joy to think about that. And determination to do all she could to make that happen.

The scrape of a chair across the floor was followed by the ominous creak of unfolding stairs.

It didn't matter. She was ready to go. With her legs

clamped tightly around the box with the baby, she pushed off to follow Cal's path into the snowy night.

Where were Abby and the baby? Cal cupped his hand above his eyes and looked toward the hill.

He could see no sign of the second sled. He raised his eyes to the triangular A-frame of the bank building and to the skylight opening in the roof. They weren't there, either, so he scanned the row of pines in the section where the ground leveled out. Nothing.

So, where could they be?

He could think of several possibilities, none of them good. He flexed his fingers in frustration, wishing he could set off in search of her. But his first concern was getting Isobel to the hospital, and to that end, he needed to turn his attention back to the road. It was only a matter of time before someone stopped to offer assistance.

"Cal? Is everything okay?" Isobel's hushed voice tensed through the cold night air. It had been a long, jarring ride down the hill, and she was visibly shaken by the ordeal. He had covered her with all of the blankets from the sled and found a place for her in a protected spot under a scrubby pine, well out of sight from the road.

He had kept only a thin yellow cloth which he draped around his neck.

"Shouldn't they be here by now?" Isobel asked, her voice breaking.

"I'm sure they'll arrive any moment." He looked from right to left every few seconds, shifting his eyes to monitor both sides of the road. Finally, in the distance, he could see the yellow glow of headlights heading east in his direction.

As the vehicle got closer, he recognized that it was a semi. And it was moving fast.

He pulled the blanket from around his neck and stepped forward onto the shoulder. He knew a rig of that size couldn't stop on a dime. But he leaned forward and waved the yellow cloth back and forth above his head.

With a spray of pebbles, the truck cruised past him in a blur.

Seconds later, the high-pitched squeal of air brakes split the air, and the semi rolled to a stop.

The driver's door shot open, and a man in a Minnesota Twins ball cap stepped out of the cab. He was bearded and burly, and the first thing he did when his boots hit the ground was spit out a mouthful of seeds.

"What's going on?" The older man's voice was thick as gravel, but his eyes were kind. "I reckon you were trying to get my attention by waving that blanket in the wind."

Cal bent over against the cab, struggling to catch his breath after racing to meet him along the side of the road. "My name is Cal Stanek. I'm the Sheriff of Dagger Lake County. My badge is in my car at the top of that hill, so you'll have to take my word for it. I won't go into all of the details, but I need to use your cell phone."

The driver hesitated a second before reaching into his pocket and handing him his phone.

Cal punched in three numbers. Linette Mae Brady answered on the first ring.

"Nine-one-one dispatch. How may I direct your call?"

"Linette, this is Cal," he said, trying hard to keep his words from getting clumped together in his mouth.

"Hey, Sheriff. I thought you were going fishing—"

He cut her off before she could say more. "I need immediate backup to assist with an incident at the Keystone Bank. Three, possibly four, armed robbers may be on the run somewhere outside the building, and a line of explosives inside that could go off at any time. First responders should approach with extreme caution."

He took another deep breath and shifted his eyes toward the truck driver who was standing a few feet away from him. Could he trust this stranger? He needed to make a split-second decision, relying only on limited observation and gut instinct. But, as a point of fact, he didn't have much choice. It would take at least fifteen minutes before an ambulance arrived, and that would be fifteen minutes too long. Isobel required immediate medical care. Her lips were blue, and her legs were trembling. The adrenaline rush that had kept her going this far had clearly run its course.

He made his decision.

"One more thing, Linette. I need for you to call North Memorial Medical Center and tell them to be expecting a gentleman named…" He waited for the driver to provide his name.

"Carl Nisswandt," the man said.

"Carl Nisswandt," Cal repeated. "He's driving an eighteen-wheeler, and they need to be ready when he pulls it into the emergency drop-off. With him will be

Isobel Carrolls. Patient gave birth less than an hour ago and may be in shock."

"Copy that," the dispatcher answered. "I've sent out a call for assistance at the bank, and I will notify the hospital immediately."

"Thanks." He ended the connection and handed the phone back to its owner.

"Mr. Nisswandt," he said with a brief nod. "Up ahead, under a pine tree, where you passed me on the road, there is the young woman who needs to be transported to the hospital. I know that these big rigs are difficult to back up, so it would be best if we both went to talk to her."

"Can do," the driver said. "It's a privilege and an honor to help law enforcement in any way."

Isobel staggered out to meet them as they approached the tall pine. "Cal. Where's Abby? Is my little boy okay?"

"Isobel. This is Mr. Nisswandt. I've asked him to take you to the hospital while I wait for Abby and the baby. When they do, I'll make sure they join you, first thing."

"But Abby said that she would be right behind us when we left. And she has my baby."

"I know. And I promise that I'll find them as soon as I can. But right now, we need to make certain that you're okay."

Isobel's body pitched forward as he helped her onto the sled. And as for Carl Nisswandt, he felt increasingly comfortable with his decision to leave Isobel in his care.

The burly truck driver made easy work of pulling Isobel down the shoulder toward the cab.

Cal stood by the side of the road and watched as the taillights of the big rig disappeared around the bend. Then he turned and began to walk toward the hill.

Within ten minutes, Isobel would be admitted to North Memorial Medical Center where she would receive the medical treatment she needed. The thought brought him some small comfort.

But it wasn't enough. Not by a long shot. There were two people still out there. Abby and the baby. And there were three armed kidnappers on the loose.

Cal's eyes skimmed from left to right across the frozen terrain. Where were they?

Granted Abby's sled was lighter, but that couldn't have delayed her more than a minute, especially if she pushed off as soon as the first sled had cleared the roof. But over a quarter of an hour had passed since he and Isobel had launched from the attic. What could have happened to cause the delay?

He was confident in the strength of the barricade he had constructed in front of the break room door. With all the shims and furniture stacked in place, it ought to have taken at least five minutes for Ricky and his minions to break through. Unless…

A troubling thought crept into his consciousness. What if the kidnappers figured out what was going on? Ricky was smart, he'd give him that. He had to be in order to plan such an elaborate scheme. If Ricky realized that there was a skylight in the attic, he might have rushed outside and stopped the second sled before it even hit the ground.

He shook his head. This line of thinking wasn't helping. He needed to find Abby and the baby before Ricky and his henchmen exacted their revenge. For the moment, he was going to assume that Abby had made it out of the attic. Where she had gone after that was the question.

It was hard to know since he himself hadn't followed a straight line to the bottom of the hill. He had veered his sled toward the trees for maximum cover, expecting Abby to follow. But if she had traveled in a different direction, she could be almost anywhere.

The sky had clouded over, and snow was coming down now in huge flakes, leaving wet blotches on his canvas jacket and chilling him to the bone. He needed to get above the trees so he could see more of the terrain.

Fists clenched with determination, he began to run.

SIX

Abby rocked back and forth as she tried to jiggle forward, but the plastic sled only sank deeper into the drift. It felt like she was sitting on a frozen boulder, covered with a chilly quilt. Already, icy dampness was seeping into her too-tight shoes and cutting off her circulation. She was cold and wet and only halfway down the hill. And now her sled was stuck.

On the bright side, the baby was warm in the crate, under a cocoon of blankets and blissfully asleep. She looped the sled's towrope around her wrist and set off toward the road. But the drifts were deeper than she expected. With every stride, it felt like she was taking one step forward and one step back.

Good thing Cal wasn't around to witness the debacle. It would probably cause him to come up with yet another story, one intended to inspire her to keep calm and carry on. She allowed herself a small smile as she stumbled forward, heading toward what she hoped was the road. It was amusing—and slightly adorable—to think about Cal's little history lesson about John Glenn.

But really, it seemed to have been effective in clearing the air—the two of them had managed to work together to engineer a successful escape.

Abby took a long step forward, pleased that she was finally gaining traction in the slippery snow. It was slow going, but after hours spent confined to a small space, it felt liberating to stretch her legs. And it was a relief to put this day behind her. She paused for a moment to absorb the reality of the last several hours. Despite unlikely odds, she was alive.

Well, she wouldn't be safe until she reached the highway. But which way to go? The usual markers in the landscape were masked with a heavy mantle of snow, and it was likely that she was headed in the wrong direction.

Should she call out Cal's name in the hope that he might answer? It was a tempting thought. But a moment later, she heard the drone of an engine and caught sight of a vehicle moving down the driveway, two pools of yellow lights marking the way. Had Ricky—and his underlings—figured out what was happening and set off on the chase? Her thoughts flashed to Cal and Isobel. With the storm continuing to rage, they might still be waiting by the road. She suppressed a shiver, panic surging through her. She needed to stay as quiet as possible and keep her body low. At least the sled she was pulling behind her was light enough to skim over the drifts. And the blankets she had tucked around her tiny passenger were thick enough to keep him warm and dry. With her shoulders hunched, she trudged forward. Each breath she took was stinging and hard, but she willed her legs to keep moving.

Suddenly, the air was pierced by the squeal of brakes and the slamming of doors, followed by the rabble of voices lashing through the wind.

The kidnappers must have spotted her and realized that she had the baby. Fresh terror reared up within her. There was nowhere to hide, nowhere to go. She looked down at the tiny newborn in the crate on the sled. A feeling of overwhelming love coursed through her veins. She would protect him. Or die trying.

"There she is," Ricky's angry voice cried out as heavy footsteps crunched through the snow. And from the sound of it, he was closing in fast.

Run! Run! She tried to lengthen her stride, but it was hard to make any headway through the knee-high drifts.

But wait! Were her eyes deceiving her? She blinked. There, in the distance, a familiar figure, covered head to toe in a mantle of snow, raced toward her. *Cal!* She had never been so glad to see someone in her life.

He ran toward her and lifted the baby from the crate. Bending his foot, he kicked aside the wooden box and then turned the front of the sled to face the hill below.

"Hop on," he said.

She dropped to her knees and settled down against the plastic as Cal placed the infant on her lap, then bent his arms against the back of the sled and pushed, propelling them forward toward the slope.

Pop! Pop!

Bullets snarled through the air as Cal jumped on the

sled behind them. With the added weight, the momentum shifted, and the sled picked up speed, skidding across the ice toward a wall of whiteness.

Abby pressed the baby tightly to her chest as thick flakes swirled against her face. The clamor of frantic cries echoed behind them. But they were moving even faster now, almost flying across the ground.

Thud! The sled hit something large and hard. A stump? Her body jolted upward and pitched to the side. She could feel Cal's movements behind her, shifting his weight to keep them from getting knocked off course.

She gasped as the surface dropped out from under them. A second later, they were flying through the air and then crashing to the ground, nailing the landing.

They were almost at the tree line now. Ahead were rows and rows of pines, but the paths between them were narrow, littered with fallen branches and decaying stumps.

"Watch out!" Cal called out.

She clutched the baby closer, but the warning came too late to prevent a branch from slapping against her face. A rush of blood surged to her cheeks, but the cold quickly numbed her pain.

And then, after the hurry and tumult, a strange sort of quietness filled the air. She realized with a start that she could no longer hear the shouts of their pursuers. The sled had skimmed across the ice into the shelter of the forest, and, at least for the moment, Ricky and the others seemed to have given up the chase.

We're safe. She breathed out a long breath she didn't

know that she had been holding. But her sigh turned into a scream as a large pine appeared in front of them. Cal leaned to the right to change their trajectory, but the sled continued to hurtle in a collision course with the tree.

Her eyes clung to the sight with terrified fascination as the pine loomed closer and closer. There was nothing to do but pray.

"Hang on!" Cal said as the sled upended, and they tumbled sideways into a drift. Instinctively, she pulled the infant against her body, bracing her forearms into a protective shield.

"Please, God. Help us," she whispered as she hit the ground and rolled onto her side, her arms instinctively cradling the baby's tiny head.

"Abby! Are you all right?" Cal reached out his hand, and she placed her own in his as he pulled her to her feet. "Is the baby okay?"

She stared down at the infant in her arms. He sniffled and huffed. Opened his tiny rosebud mouth to pull in a breath. His lips tucked upward in a sad sort of smile. And then he fell back asleep.

Piling the extra blankets, Cal made a cozy nest, designed to keep their tiny traveling companion safe and warm. It lacked the sturdy protection of the crate, but it would do for the time being. And they could move faster if they didn't have to trade off carrying the baby. They might even make it back to the highway before Ricky and his flunkies could follow their tracks.

He grasped the rope and gave it a firm pull. He took two steps forward, then slowed his pace to wait for Abby.

"What's the plan here, Cal?" Abby said, falling in next to him as they trudged through the pines.

He wished he knew. "At this point, the only plan is to put as much space as we can between us and the kidnappers."

"At least Isobel is safe." Abby's smile collapsed into a frown. "At least I hope so."

"I expect that she's already checked in at the hospital. The trucker who stopped to help us seemed like a good guy. And Isobel was so weak at that point that I didn't have much choice. Assuming the nine-one-one dispatcher managed to patch a call through to the station, a dozen or so deputies will soon be arriving at the bank."

"But Ricky and the others won't be there."

"That's true. But the authorities will realize what happened and send off a search party to comb the area."

They were quiet for a minute. The only sound was the crunch of their shoes against the snow.

"So," Abby said at last. "You're probably wondering what happened with my sled."

When he didn't answer, she continued.

"I thought I was following along the path you left, but I ended up spinning sideways in the wrong direction. Then I got stuck in a snowdrift, and it all went 9-shaped from there."

"Not your fault. The snow was a lot slicker than I expected."

"But if I had kept control and hadn't veered off your

path, we wouldn't be stuck out here with the baby, lost in the woods."

"We're not lost. We're in the process of finding our way. Besides—" he shrugged "—when it comes to mistakes, I seem to have cornered the market, starting with my decision to leave my cell phone in the truck. And I should have realized that Max and Martina's plans involved something a lot more devious than robbing the bank."

Abby reached over and touched the sleeve of his coat. "Well, Cal, I suppose we both made mistakes. But you were the one who ended up saving the day. We were out of options when you found those sleds. Escaping through the skylight was a genius plan. You deserve all the credit for rescuing Isobel and the baby."

"It was a team effort," he said.

They walked awhile in silence. He shot another quick glance at Abby as she trudged along next to him. "You still doing okay?"

She caught his eye and smiled back at him.

"I'm good," she said.

Good? That was putting a positive spin on it. She had to be freezing. The shoes he had found for her in the attic were thin and flimsy, unlike his own insulated footwear. How much longer could she go before she began to show the signs of frostbite? Numbness, pain and swelling. Fever and the inability to move. He could only hope it wouldn't come to that.

He turned again to face her. "I know you don't want to complain, but your feet must be really cold. Maybe you should ride on the sled next to the baby. Just for a while. You could use one of the blankets to warm up your legs."

"Cal?" Abby raised her voice to be heard over the wind. "I appreciate your concern, but I'm really am fine at the moment. I promise to tell you if I feel the start of frostbite. The trainers you found in the attic were a titch too small, so I slipped on an extra pair of socks that I found in a drawer in the break room. And I actually have another trick for keeping myself distracted. I've been thinking about Davey and the first thing I want to do when I bring him home to live with me. Did I tell you that I bought him a bike? I saw it on Craigslist, and it was the perfect size. It has training wheels and everything."

Davey, of course. He was learning that when Abby decided to do something, she didn't proceed with any halfway measures.

"That's great, Abby. And if you need some help teaching him to ride without the extra wheels, I'd be glad to oblige. It would be fun to pay it forward for all the time my own dad spent running behind me holding on to the seat of my bike until I felt ready to strike out on my own."

Abby grinned. "I just might take you up on that."

He hoped that she did. He'd be glad to lend a hand any way he could. If things had gone differently with Shannon, he might've had a little boy like Davey to call his own.

A wave of melancholy engulfed his senses. Why was it that grief never seemed to hit him straight on?

Instead, it crept around unexpected corners, bent on knocking him flat. He shook his head, determined not to allow sadness to overtake him. He was usually an optimistic person. He didn't even think about Shannon all that much anymore. So why was she on his mind so much tonight?

He knew the answer even before he posed that question.

It was because of Abby. And how much she reminded him of his wife.

It wasn't just Abby's posh appearance—the designer clothes and the perfectly coiffed hair. It was something deeper, something that he had noticed just a couple of weeks into his job as sheriff.

Arriving on the scene of a fatal accident, he had watched Abby's desperate attempts to revive the driver, even after it was clear to everyone present that the man had stopped breathing and was gone. Over and over again, she'd administered CPR, pushing hard and fast against the man's chest, not stopping until she was pulled off by one of the medics. Dedication like that was to be admired, but over time, he had seen how that sort of single-minded determination became Shannon's undoing in her career as an officer on the force. And how it had ultimately resulted in their decision to separate and then divorce.

He had gotten to know Abby pretty well during the past few hours, and he had to admit that those sorts of comparisons to Shannon weren't quite fair. Abby was determined and, courageous, but not to the point of being foolhardy. Abby was... He searched his mind for the best description, finally settling on empathetic and caring. In fact, the more he thought about it, the more he realized that Abby wasn't much like Shannon at all.

But he'd been down a long, hard road when his marriage imploded, and all his hopes for the future were lost.

And he wasn't sure he was ready to take on anything like that again.

SEVEN

It was snowing harder now, and the trail was becoming increasingly difficult to navigate. Large, heavy flurries were leaking from the treetops, through the branches and onto the ground as a stiff west wind wiped away their footprints almost as quickly as they were made.

Abby paused to stare at the felled pine blocking their path. Wasn't that the same tree they'd passed a half hour ago? It couldn't be. Could it? She traced her gaze toward Cal, who was walking beside her. His eyes seemed troubled, and she wondered if, like her, he suspected that they were walking in circles, past the same snow-covered landmarks again and again.

She shot him what she hoped was an encouraging smile. "It shouldn't be much longer before we emerge from the trees. And once we get to the road, we'll flag down someone passing by and hitch a ride into town."

"I don't know, Abby." He stopped to gaze at a cluster of pines ahead. "It's hard to tell in the shelter of these tall pines, but the blizzard seems to be picking up steam. Not many folks are apt to be out and about in this kind of weather."

"Maybe. But all we need is one driver to stop and give us a ride. And isn't there a chance that the inclement weather has scared off Ricky and the others? Is there a chance they decided to take the money they stole from the bank and head for home?"

Cal shook his head. "It's possible. But my gut tells me they're still out there. I don't know where, but I don't think that they've abandoned the chase. Ricky doesn't seem like the kind of person who gives up easily."

"But don't you think that…" She paused midsentence as a boom reverberated in the distance. "What was that?"

"Not sure. It sounded like it came from somewhere up ahead."

A second blast rumbled. The baby stirred and began to cry.

Abby bent down and lifted the baby off the sled. "I'm going to hold the little guy for a bit, just until he calms down. I've missed having him in my arms."

"Okay. We can trade off carrying him. The gap between the trees is so narrow that it might be best to abandon the sled."

Abby nodded. The thud of the infant's heartbeat beside her own was the motivation she needed to keep going, putting one foot in front of the other as she plodded through the drifts. She didn't want to think about booms and blasts that shattered the silence of the night. And she didn't want to think about Ricky and the other kidnappers lying in wait somewhere around the bend.

Cal moved forward and took the lead. She stepped in his oversize footprints as he wove his way through the trees and across the uneven terrain. It was slow going. Her legs were tired, and her feet were cold. But that didn't matter. She and Cal had jobs to do. They were in this together. It helped to think of their trek as part and parcel of their everyday duties, their commitment to saving lives and protecting the innocent.

It had been clever of Cal to steer the sled into the trees where the SUVs wouldn't be able to follow them. It evened the playing field, but only a bit. Growing up, she had known this forest like the back of her hand, but with the storm raging all around them, she lacked the certainty to navigate the way. It was almost impossible to recognize her usual landmarks under this much snow.

Tears prickled at the backs of her eyes, but she blinked them away. Hadn't God already provided for them? Isobel's labor had been straightforward. The baby was healthy, and so far, they had kept him out of Ricky's clutches. Isobel was probably at the hospital, hooked up to an IV. The authorities were alerted to the situation. She breathed in slowly to steady her racing heart.

"Thank you, God," she whispered. "But please, help and guide us as we try to preserve this brand-new life."

"Hey, hey, hey!" Cal's excited voice broke through her thoughts. "Look what I found."

She hurried the few paces toward the spot where he was standing. Cal brushed aside a coating of flakes to reveal a rectangular plaque that had been hammered onto the trunk of a tall pine. "Hope Trail," she read. "And the arrow is pointing straight ahead." A glimmer of joy sparked in her chest. "I know this path! It isn't the easiest or straightest route, but it leads to the scenic overlook of Highway 101! And, if memory serves, we'll reach it in less than an hour."

Cal scratched his chin and his lips curved into a half smile. "Highway 101, you said? Isn't there a gas station a short distance from the overlook? A couple of pumps out front and a small convenience store in the back? Maybe we should stop there and see if we can call for help. It would be a good place to hole up and wait for reinforcements."

Of course. One Duck Shop. She knew it well.

"Here, let me take the little guy." Cal reached out his arms. "You need a rest."

Abby peeked down again. She didn't want to hand over the baby, but Cal was right. Her arms were stiffening up. Reluctantly, she passed the wrapped bundle to Cal. He unzipped his coat, folded one arm against his chest and then zipped it back up. With the baby's little head popping out from the top of the zipper, Cal made easy work of his role of guardian and protector.

"All right," he said. "We can walk quickly, but we shouldn't rush. We can't afford to stumble over a fallen branch and break a leg."

Abby nodded. As much as she wanted to take off sprinting down the path, it wouldn't help to be reckless. "Since you have the baby, let me go first."

She started forward. She had assumed that walking along the path would be easier than wandering through the forest, but the snow was thicker here, and the drifts were even larger than the ones near the trees. And heavy flakes were still coming down, obstructing her visibility. She could see three, maybe four feet ahead. She put her right arm out in front of her, and her left arm to the side, feeling for encroaching branches. As long as they stayed on the path, they would be fine. A few times, as she stepped forward, her hands brushed against the sharp needles of a nearby pine, and she would veer sideways away from the trees. Behind her, she could hear Cal's heavy breathing. She was grateful that he was carrying the baby. All of her energy was channeled into navigating the trail.

Behind her, Cal started to hum a song, and she smiled as she listened, trying to identify the melody. After a few more notes, she had it. "Baby Beluga," an old favorite of hers and her brother, Gideon, when they were growing up.

"Hey," she said, slowing down so he could catch up and walk beside her. "I know that tune. My dad used to sing it to us whenever we visited the zoo."

"Your dad, huh? I haven't met him, so I assume he doesn't live on the reservation."

"No. He died when I was ten. He was driving me to camp when a semi came out of nowhere and plowed into our car. It was horrible. But the paramedics at the scene were amazing. I decided then and there that I'd found my future career."

If "horrible" described the accident, then "devastating heartbreak" would sum up the aftermath. Even now, twenty-five years later, the memory was still fresh. The emergency responders had arrived within minutes of the call. One of them lifted her out of the car and wrapped her in a blanket and then sat with her and waited while the rest of the crew tried to revive her dad. They did everything they could to save him, but he never regained consciousness. He'd died in the ambulance on the way to the hospital.

Her mom had a tough time dealing with the loss, retreating into a shell of sadness and despair. There were days when there wasn't anything to eat in the refrigerator or any clean clothes to wear. Bills piled up, and creditors called all hours of the day. It was a dark, dismal couple of months for all of them.

That was when she had first realized the negative side of loving someone, the feelings of helplessness and abandonment that came with loss. But, unlike her mother who had managed her grief by retreating from the world, Abby had accepted her new responsibilities with grim determination. Self-reliance became her coping mechanism.

She could still recall announcing to her fourth-grade class that she would never get married because she was never going to fall in love. If riding her bike was any indication, falling was a painful experience, one that she didn't care to repeat.

Besides, her life, even as a ten-year-old, was already too full, between minding her younger brother and managing the house. Well-meaning neighbors had tried to help. So had the principal from her school and the social workers who had begun paying weekly visits to their ramshackle house. But it wasn't until her uncle pulled up in front of their house with an empty U-Haul and a plan to take them to Dagger Lake that things took a turn for the better.

Abby used the back of her glove to wipe away a tear.

"I still miss him, even after all this time. I guess the way he died, with me there in the car with him, will be etched on my heart forever."

"It must have been awful." Cal's voice was soft and comforting.

"It was for a long while. But there were unexpected blessings, too. We ended up moving back to the reservation, and I got to spend time with my brother. Before that, there were so many distractions keeping us apart. But in Dagger Lake, we bonded over our love of the outdoors and of fishing. Almost every weekend, we headed to the lake and cast out our lines."

"Mmm. A fresh caught walleye sounds really good right now."

"Maybe when we get home, you can come over for supper, and I can show off my skills with a frying pan and a bunch of fresh herbs."

Abby tucked away a smile and planted her eyes on the ground. Had she really just invited Cal over to her house for dinner? It was a normal gesture of friendship, so why not? Cal had been nothing short of kind since the first moment they arrived at the bank. And when she told him about the adoption, he had been unfailingly positive in his support. And yet… Cal claimed that he was interested in clearing the air and making a new start. Should she risk asking him about a couple of remarks he had made during his first few months in Dagger Lake?

She pressed her lips together and decided to go for it. "So, Cal. I'm really happy that we decided to be friends, especially given all that we've been through together tonight. But there is one thing…" She paused. Her grievances seemed so petty, but his comments still rankled. "When you first came to town, I overheard you referring to me as a fashionista."

"Hmm," Cal said. "That happened so long ago I can hardly remember. But I suppose I was surprised about the high heels you sometimes wore to work. But honestly, Abby? You need to cut me some slack here. The paramedics I worked with on my last job wore gray jumpsuits, and you always looked so posh and pulled together. Besides, how was I to know that you were skulking in the shadows, committing my offhand remarks to memory?"

"First of all, I wasn't 'skulking' anywhere. I was standing by my car, so you should have realized that I could hear everything you said."

"I'm sorry," he said. "I didn't actually realize you heard me, but I agree that was rude."

Abby pulled in a deep breath and let it out slowly. Cal didn't know it, but that particular remark wasn't the only negative comment of his that she had overheard in the weeks after he had arrived in town.

The very next week after he had made that fashionista comment, she had also heard him refer to her home town as a Podunk place that rolled up the sidewalks at 7 p.m.

Okay. Looking back, she'd concede that maybe her reaction was a bit thin-skinned. But she loved Dagger Lake. She had grown up here, and years ago, members of the tribal community had funded a scholarship to help her become a paramedic. Without their assistance, she'd still be waiting tables at the local diner with no chance of achieving her dream. No wonder she felt defensive when anyone disparaged her hometown.

And as much as she loved it, she knew that Dagger Lake wasn't everyone's cup of tea. In fact, it sometimes felt as if the place was shrinking right before her eyes as more and more people picked up and moved away. A handful of her cousins had left town. So had her favorite teacher from high school and her first partner on the job. They had all gone in search of better opportunities in bigger cities in the Midwest. Fargo. Minneapolis. Sioux Falls. It was easy to imagine, given Cal's remarks, that he would be quick to follow.

"Now that you've been in town for two years, do you plan to stick around?"

He shot her a look. "I just bought a house, so it looks like it. Why?"

"Just wondering," she said. "Because I also sort of overheard you say that Dagger Lake was a Podunk place that was out in the sticks."

Cal chuckled softly. "Did I really say that? Well, it's true, isn't it? But that doesn't mean I don't like it here. I like it a lot. And I certainly didn't intend to hurt your feelings by criticizing your town."

She couldn't hide the smile forming on her lips. "No problem. I just wanted to clear the air."

"Consider it cleared. Is that it? Or are there any other comments of mine that you just happened to overhear? I hate to think that there might be a whole, long list of goofy things I said when I didn't think anyone was listening."

"No. That's it. I just wanted to go forward with a clean slate since we're planning to be good friends."

"*Good* friends, huh? Glad to hear that I've been promoted. But I've got to say that you have me wondering if my tendency to talk without thinking was the reason you didn't show up for our date?"

Abby flushed. "No. I told you. I canceled because of what was happening with Davey." She smiled. "But those comments did make it easier to flake out without offering an excuse."

Cal shook his head. "Well, let me say once again that I'm very sorry for being so thoughtless. It's something I've been working on in the past year. I've been trying to stop shooting off my mouth at the slightest provocation. Please accept my apology on both counts."

"Consider it done," she said. "And I hope you'll agree to forgive me for leaving you waiting at the restaurant."

"Absolutely," he said. "The way it worked out was probably for the best."

"Agreed," she said.

So that was that, then. They were both on the same page. Cal wasn't interested in a romantic relationship, and neither was she. But how to explain the strange feeling of disappointment pinging in her heart?

But she couldn't think about that now as the path narrowed again, and Cal stepped back to walk behind her, allowing her to once again lead the way.

It was eerie being out in the woods with just Cal and the baby. After so many hours trapped in the bank, the adrenaline rush of Isobel's labor and delivery and the frantic escape through the roof, the hushed stillness of the forest was unnerving. Each step was slow and laborious, but she steadied her breathing and persevered. She could feel her blood coursing through her body, and her heart thudded in her chest. Her limbs ached from the exertion, but at least she was no longer cold. A thin sheen of sweat clung to her arms and legs. The warmth was an odd sensation, especially since she could barely feel her toes.

The strangeness of the experience served to tighten her resolve about her plans for the future. Once things got back to normal—once the kidnappers were apprehended and the baby was safe—she'd follow through on her invitation to have Cal over for dinner. Even though neither of them was interested in dating, that didn't mean that they couldn't become friends.

Wow. If twenty-four hours ago, someone had told her that she would actually be looking forward to spending time with Cal Stanek, she wouldn't have believed it. But, now, it was hard to remember how awkward things used to be between them.

Some of the blame for that could be fixed on her brother and several other well-meaning acquaintances who had micromanaged that unsuccessful first date. Though she supposed she couldn't blame them for trying. There had been an initial attraction, at least on her part. The first time she had seen Cal, he was standing on her brother Gideon's dock, holding a stringer of perch in his outstretched hand. She had heard rumors about the new Sheriff in town, that he was tall, dark and handsome. Easy on the eyes, if you liked the type. She wasn't sure about that, but she certainly had been intrigued when her brother invited her over to meet his new friend.

And Cal sure did make a good first impression. Dark hair, keen eyes and a killer smile that made her feel like she was the most fascinating person in the world. The cotton tee he was wearing did nothing to hide his broad shoulders and strong arms. And when he stepped forward to shake her hand, a jolt of electricity had shot through her fingertips.

Of course, that wasn't enough to alter her view of marriage or romance. Especially in the weeks that followed their first meeting on the dock when Cal's thoughtless comments caused her to become even more wary of the widowed sheriff. But, now, those feelings of guardedness had been put to rest, and she was grateful for Cal's support of her decision to adopt Davey Lightfoot.

Still, she couldn't help but worry that she was getting ahead of herself, talking so much about Davey. If only she could be sure the adoption would really happen. It would be wonderful to finally bring Davey home, though it wouldn't be without its challenges. Davey had been diagnosed with a few learning issues, which would require constant attention and care. But she knew all that when she filed her application. And she was all in on being there for Davey.

Her own mom had not been an especially good role model. Darla Marshall had never been a particularly maternal person, but without the anchor of her husband, she abandoned all parental responsibilities. Not that Abby completely blamed her. It had to be a challenge to lose a spouse, to have her whole world destroyed and to start over as a widow with two young kids. But if her mother had taught her anything, it was what not to do, and she was determined to harness everything in her power to be a real parent for Davey. Between her job and her new son, her life would be full.

She took a deep breath and pushed forward. The trek through the forest had been a long slog with no end in sight, and she was starting to feel discouraged. Had she really told Cal that they would reach the road in less than sixty minutes? It felt like they had been walking hours. She wanted to turn around and offer to take the baby, but she forced herself to forge ahead.

Then, suddenly, without warning, the ground evened out, and her feet gave out from under her as she pitched forward into a wide drift of wind-tossed snow.

"Are you hurt?" Cal stood above her, looking down.

She laughed. "Not at all. It was a soft landing." She lay still for a moment, enjoying the plush pillow of flakes that had cushioned her fall. It felt good to rest. But the sound of the soft cries coming from the bundle in Cal's arms snapped her back to reality. Her senses charged to high alert as she glanced up and realized that they were no longer under the canopy of the trees. Without realizing what was happening, she had tumbled down the last few feet of the trail and landed on the shoulder of Highway 101.

"Look!" She pulled herself up, brushed the snow off her coat and pointed toward the road. "We did it!"

"You did it."

Tears of gratitude stung her eyes. She turned around

and smiled at Cal, or rather a snow-covered shape that resembled the sheriff. White flakes clung to his jacket and pants and even the stubble along his face and jaw. But his eyes blazed back at her with eagerness and impatience.

"Let's go find shelter," he said with a smile. He charged forward with renewed energy, as if the treacherous journey through the woods had not winded him at all. She let him take the lead, grateful for the respite. Pulling in a deep breath, she summoned up her last bit of stamina and followed him down the road.

Abby had done it. She had led them through a blinding snowstorm and along the steep path to the road. Cal glanced backward, and noticing that she was a few paces behind, he slowed his stride so she could catch up. She had to be exhausted. He certainly was. His legs throbbed, and his left arm was cramped and stiff from holding the baby. But he had also never felt more alive.

And right here. Right now. This was his clarifying moment. He felt content. He felt sure that God had a plan to keep them safe for the journey ahead. He was going to give his all to protect the baby in his arms and the feisty woman trudging behind him.

He turned his head again. Abby's head was bent low as her feet followed his footsteps along the road. Snow clung to her dark hair, and she looked almost fragile against the desolate landscape. As if reading his thoughts, she lifted her head and caught his stare. She squared her shoulders and raised her chin.

Cal turned back around. Message received. She was just as tough as he was. Which he knew already.

Wait! He froze. What was that? The low hum of an approaching vehicle caught his ear. His heart jack-knifed in his chest.

"Abby! Quick! We need to take cover!"

"What?" Her eyes were focused downward at the ground under their feet.

"Cover! Now!" He grabbed her hand and pulled her toward the side of the embankment. He shot a quick glance back toward the road. Would the driver notice their footprints? No. The gusting wind had already dusted the tarmac with enough snow to cover their tracks.

He handed Abby the baby and crouched down beside her.

"Ricky," she whispered. The word cut like a dagger in the cold, night air.

The whir of an engine splintered through the stillness of the night. The vehicle would be passing them at any moment. The drifts at the top of the gully provided sufficient cover to allow them to watch for approaching headlights. Cal tensed his legs, ready to rush toward the road and flag down a vehicle other than a black SUV.

A second later, the icy tarmac was illuminated by a black Land Rover. Even at a distance, he could see the tinted windows and the out-of-state front plates. The SUV was coasting along slowly, and its speed diminished as it approached their hiding spot. He racked his brain to anticipate every eventuality. If the vehicle stopped, Abby should run toward the forest while he tried to buy them time. Doing what he wasn't certain. His free hand dug into the snow and searched for something, anything, he could use as a weapon. His fingers closed around a large rock. He gripped the stone, waiting for the telltale crunch of tires pulling to the side of the road. After a few more seconds, the drone of the engine grew fainter, and the beams of the headlights disappeared from sight. He waited a moment longer and then sat up.

Abby pulled herself up next to him, clutching the baby tightly in her arms.

"They didn't see us. But what are the chances that they'll guess where we're headed?"

He had been wondering the same thing. He glanced down at the baby. There was a bluish hue to his nose and cheeks.

"The pumps aren't lit up or operational. And the convenience store isn't visible from the highway. There's a good chance they'll pass it by and not see a thing." He sounded a lot more confident than he felt. But he wanted to focus on the positive. "We can only hope that they're headed north, and if they circle back, they'll choose to follow another road. No matter what, we need to get this little guy out of the cold and warm him up."

"Here. Wait a moment." Abby bent down and scooped up a handful of snow, cupped her hands together and held them toward the infant. The baby screwed his mouth into a look of displeasure as the cold wetness came in contact with his face. But a moment later, his lips pursed out and he began to suck at the snow in Abby's hand. They waited a few minutes until he had finished drinking, and then Abby brushed her hands off.

"It isn't as good as mother's milk, but it will keep him from getting dehydrated."

Cal nodded. His heart was still thudding in his chest, but it was hard to tell whether it was from their narrow escape or from observing Abby's tenderness.

"Right, let's keep going." His voice sounded husky to his own ears. A moment later, he paused and pointed toward a building in the distance. "Look. At long last, we've reached our destination."

There was no sign on the outside, but everyone in Dagger Lake knew the gray-bricked, one-story building as One Duck Shop, convenience store and gas station all in one. The place looked deserted with no sign of a black Land Rover anywhere near.

Still, it was best to be careful.

There was always the chance that the driver had parked the vehicle somewhere down the road and that Ricky and the others were inside the store, lying in wait.

And if that was the case, he needed to stay alert and be ready. He held fast to the stone in his hand. It would hardly be effective against the kidnappers' guns, but it was the best he could do at the moment.

EIGHT

Abby followed behind Cal as they made their way up the slippery embankment toward the road. Twenty yards ahead of them, the snow-covered gas pumps of One Duck Shop beckoned them forward like ghostly sentinels guarding the station. The coast seemed to be clear, at least for the moment. Trailing behind Cal, she quickened her steps as they approached the front of the store.

Cal put a hand on her arm and gestured toward the woodpile by the far side of the building. "You take the baby and wait over there while I check for fresh tracks around the perimeter."

"Okay," she breathed back. "The store closed at seven last night, and it won't open back up again until nine in the morning. The pumps are shut down for the night, so no one should be around. But be careful. Okay?"

Cal turned and winked at her. She got the picture. Of course, he'd be careful. He was, after all, the sheriff.

She crouched down next to the woodpile and watched for Cal's signal. It was hard to believe that only yesterday, she had stopped here for gas on the way into town to run a couple of errands. At the time, she was waiting for a status report of her petition to adopt Davey Lightfoot, so she had kept her phone within easy reach, tucked in the outer pocket of her coat.

And here she was, a little more than a dozen hours later, huddled ten feet from that same pump, still not sure what was going on with the adoption.

Her mind flashed for a minute on an image of Davey the first time they met. She had been on duty when the request came in for medical assistance for an elderly patient who had fallen down the stairs. Davey was only two years old, but with his grandfather injured and his grandmother in bed recovering from a stroke, he was the one who answered the door. There he stood, in his yellow footie pajamas, his long, dark hair falling into his huge, worried eyes. A rush of maternal love surged through her body. Most kids would have been reduced to tears by the crisis, but Davey was so brave, toddling down the hallway, clutching a tattered blanket as he led the emergency responders to the spot at the bottom of the stairs. He didn't say a word, just stood by quietly as his grandfather was loaded on a gurney.

Come to think of it, Cal had been there that night, too. In fact, he had been the one to notify Davey's social worker about the accident and to ask her to find someone to stay with the family while the grandfather recovered at the hospital. She had forgotten about that.

It had been many long months since she had shown up for that emergency call, months of paperwork and interviews, months of waiting and hoping and falling on her knees in prayer. Both sets of Davey's grandparents had officially signed over custody, reluctantly agreed that they weren't up for the task of raising the little boy. That had been an emotional day. It was too bad that the legal system required such finality in order to allow adoption to proceed. But Abby had assured them that they would always be a welcome part of Davey's life. She was ready and excited to finalize the adoption. She wanted to be a mother. And Davey needed a home.

She had always been proudly independent and confident in her own ability to deal with any problem life sent her way. Why ask for help when she could do it on her own? Proof positive could be found right here, at One Duck Shop, the site of her first job on the reservation. Hoping to make some money to help her family, she had applied for a part-time position on her fourteenth birthday and started restocking shelves the following day.

"Pssst!" A whisper slid through the stillness of the night.

A dark figure beckoned her forward. Cal. He lowered his voice to explain. "I couldn't pick the lock, so I broke a window in the back. And guess what? There's an old snowmobile parked back there, too. Once we find a phone and call the station, I might just try to hotwire the ignition to see if I can get it to work. The way I see it, it can't hurt to have a backup plan just in case we need to make a speedy exit. But for now, I think we can take our little friend to warm up inside the store. While you make sure he's comfortable, I'll see if I can find a phone and call nine-one-one."

Abby nodded. She could help with that. She knew

that Mr. Ratten, the shop's owner, kept an old-school rotary phone in front of the store.

"Here, let me take the little guy," Cal offered as they wound around to the back of the store. He hopped over the ledge of the broken window and held out his arms. Abby passed the bundle over to him and climbed over the sill.

A rush of warmth greeted her as she stepped down onto the floor. The aisles formed a shadowy labyrinth looming large in their path. But a sliver of moonlight shone through a small side window, guiding them forward to the front of the store.

"The phone is on a shelf by the door."

She followed behind Cal as he headed down the main aisle toward the front of the store. Cal lifted up the receiver, waited a moment, and then shook his head. His clenched lips and furrowed brow said it all. There was no connection. He set the phone back on the cradle and drummed his fingers against the counter, telegraphing his frustration.

"I guess we shouldn't be surprised," he said at last. "The landlines always go down during major storms, so it makes sense that a blizzard like this would have disrupted service. Is there any chance this place sells burner phones?"

She shook her head. "I don't think so."

"Okay. We'll figure something out. Let's find a couple of flashlights and check this place out."

"This way." She reached forward and felt along the side wall. Flashlights and batteries would be in the next aisle over. She turned the corner and walked a few paces toward the middle shelf. "We should both take one of those big Maglites and a smaller one, too, to keep in our pockets."

Cal ripped open a package of D batteries and slipped them into the shaft of one of the larger lights. "Here. Use this to find the little guy some food and dry clothes."

Abby nodded. "I'll be in aisle two, next to the fishing gear."

Cal called after her. "Good thing you know right where to go."

But she had already turned the corner, her legs hurrying toward the shelf devoted to an assortment of baby items and sundry goods. She snatched up a box of diapers and a package of onesies. Her eyes scanned for more. Plastic and glass bottles. She grabbed a plastic one. What about formula? The baby whimpered, and she joggled him up and down as she searched.

Aha! Relief exploded in her chest. At the very bottom of the shelf, tucked beside a selection of baby shampoos, was a box of powdered formula.

Just in time, too. The baby opened his eyes and let out a scream loud enough to quake the rafters. Isobel's little boy was awake, probably wet and cold and hungry. And she needed to fix all that before the kidnappers returned.

Cal smiled as he slipped a small flashlight and keychain in the pocket of his overalls. Despite the unhappy wailing of the littlest member of their team, he and Abby were in the best position they had been all night. They were out of the bank. They were no longer braving the snow and wind. And they had found the perfect spot to hole up until the storm passed. His eyes darted toward the restroom door. Ten minutes earlier, Abby had hurried inside, carrying the crying baby and a whole armful of stuff.

He blew out a sigh, grateful for Abby's steadying presence beside him. Not only had she saved them time by locating everything they needed, she had also taken the lead in caring for a needy newborn.

Well, she wasn't the only one who could be productive. If they were going to spend some quality time here, he needed to put some precautions in place. Unlike Abby, his knowledge of One Duck Shop was limited to the handful of times he had stopped in for gas and a cup of coffee on his way to the reservation.

Situated off the highway at the entrance of the reservation, One Duck Shop was a kind of catch-all convenience, grocery and hardware store rolled into one. And if memory served, the place sold a number of items that could be repurposed into an early warning system to alert them to the presence of intruders. He snatched up a shopping basket and headed down the aisles, tracing the beam of his flashlight over the shelves and grabbing items that could be useful for setting a trap.

After just a few minutes, his basket was overflowing. This place really was amazing. It didn't carry a wide selection of different brands, but it seemed to have just about everything he might need. He walked back to the window he had broken earlier. With masking tape and a tarp, he covered the opening and then affixed several toy bells to the plastic. If anyone tried to come in that way, the ringing would alert them of the intrusion.

From there he headed back to the front of the store. Excellent. He smiled. The main entry door opened outward. Using a pocketknife, he had found in the home repair aisle, he cut some nylon fishing line and, with a hammer and a nail, fixed it in place on the left side of the door. He pulled the string taut and did the same thing on the right side. Anyone trying to enter would trip and hit the floor. Then, he grabbed a gallon of paint from the home repair aisle. He tied more nylon fishing thread to the door and then looped it through the handle. Now he needed to find a way to hoist the whole thing above the door. He dragged over a chair, grabbed the paint can and the heavy-duty staple gun and stepped up onto the chair. With a few dozen staples holding the can in place, the trap seemed secure. He stepped down from the chair, pulled the fishing line taut and knotted it tightly against the hinge on the door.

He stepped back to consider his handiwork.

The booby trap wasn't fancy. But it would get the job done. If anyone tried to open the door, the pull on the fishing line would wrench the paint can forward. The line of staples couldn't withstand the force, and the fourteen-pound can would quickly crash down on the intruder's head.

"Smart move." Abby suddenly materialized beside him with Isobel's little boy nestled tight in her arms.

"Thanks." He turned to face her. "Our little traveling companion looks quite content."

"I know. Right?" she said. "I filled a bottle with

Loyal Readers
FREE BOOKS Voucher

We're giving away THOUSANDS

of **FREE BOOKS**

LOVE INSPIRED
INSPIRATIONAL ROMANCE

To Protect
His Children
LINDA GOODNIGHT
NEW YORK TIMES BESTSELLING AUTHOR

He'll do anything to
make sure they're
cared for

GER PRINT

Romance

LOVE INSPIRED SUSPENSE
INSPIRATIONAL ROMANCE

Alaskan
Rescue
TERRI REED

K-9 UNIT

ALASKA K-9 UNIT

LARGE

Suspense

Don't Miss
Out! Send
for Your
Free Books
Today!

Get up to 4
FREE FABULOUS BOOKS
You Love!

To thank you for being a loyal reader we'd like to send you up to 4 FREE BOOKS, absolutely free.

Just write "YES" on the Loyal Reader Voucher and we'll send you up to 4 Free Books and Free Mystery Gifts, altogether worth over $20, as a way of saying thank you for being a loyal reader.

Try **Love Inspired® Romance Larger-Print** books and fall in love with inspirational romances that take you on an uplifting journey of faith, forgiveness and hope.

Try **Love Inspired® Suspense Larger-Print** books where courage and optimism unite in stories of faith and love in the face of danger.

Or **TRY BOTH!**

We are so glad you love the books as much as we do and can't wait to send you great new books.

So don't miss out, return your Loyal Reader Voucher Today!

Pam Powers

LOYAL READER
FREE BOOKS VOUCHER

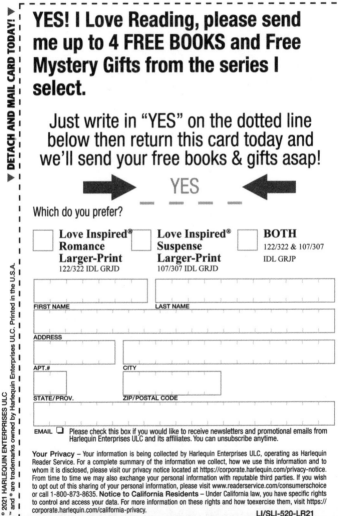

▼ DETACH AND MAIL CARD TODAY! ▼

YES! I Love Reading, please send me up to 4 FREE BOOKS and Free Mystery Gifts from the series I select.

Just write in "YES" on the dotted line below then return this card today and we'll send your free books & gifts asap!

➡ YES ⬅

Which do you prefer?

☐ **Love Inspired®
Romance
Larger-Print**
122/322 IDL GRJD

☐ **Love Inspired®
Suspense
Larger-Print**
107/307 IDL GRJD

☐ **BOTH**
122/322 & 107/307
IDL GRJP

FIRST NAME _____ LAST NAME _____

ADDRESS _____

APT.# _____ CITY _____

STATE/PROV. _____ ZIP/POSTAL CODE _____

EMAIL ☐ Please check this box if you would like to receive newsletters and promotional emails from Harlequin Enterprises ULC and its affiliates. You can unsubscribe anytime.

Your Privacy – Your information is being collected by Harlequin Enterprises ULC, operating as Harlequin Reader Service. For a complete summary of the information we collect, how we use this information and to whom it is disclosed, please visit our privacy notice located at https://corporate.harlequin.com/privacy-notice. From time to time we may also exchange your personal information with reputable third parties. If you wish to opt out of this sharing of your personal information, please visit www.readerservice.com/consumerschoice or call 1-800-873-8635. **Notice to California Residents** – Under California law, you have specific rights to control and access your data. For more information on these rights and how to exercise them, visit https://corporate.harlequin.com/california-privacy.

© 2021 HARLEQUIN ENTERPRISES ULC
™ and ® are trademarks owned by Harlequin Enterprises ULC. Printed in the U.S.A.

LI/SLI-520-LR21

♦ HARLEQUIN® Reader Service — **Here's how it works:**

Accepting your 2 free books and 2 free gifts (gifts valued at approximately $10.00 retail) places you under no obligation to buy anything. You may keep the books and gifts and return the shipping statement marked "cancel." If you do not cancel, approximately one month later we'll send you 6 more books from each series you have chosen, and bill you at our low, subscribers-only discount price. Love Inspired® Romance Larger-Print books and Love Inspired® Suspense Larger-Print books consist of 6 books each month and cost just $5.99 each in the U.S. or $6.24 each in Canada. That is a savings of at least 17% off the cover price. It's quite a bargain! Shipping and handling is just 50¢ per book in the U.S. and $1.25 per book in Canada*. You may return any shipment at our expense and cancel at any time — or you may continue to receive monthly shipments at our low, subscribers-only discount price plus shipping and handling. *Terms and prices subject to change without notice. Prices do not include sales taxes which will be charged (if applicable) based on your state or country of residence. Canadian residents will be charged applicable taxes. Offer not valid in Quebec. Books received may not be as shown. All orders subject to approval. Credit or debit balances in a customer's account(s) may be offset by any other outstanding balance owed by or to the customer. Please allow 3 to 4 weeks for delivery. Offer available while quantities last. **Your Privacy** – Your information is being collected by Harlequin Enterprises ULC, operating as Harlequin Reader Service. For a complete summary of the information we collect, how we use this information and to whom it is disclosed, please visit our privacy notice located at https://corporate.harlequin.com/privacy-notice. From time to time we may also exchange your personal information with reputable third parties. If you wish to opt out of this sharing of your personal information, please visit www.readerservice.com/consumerschoice or call 1-800-873-8635. **Notice to California Residents** – Under California law, you have specific rights to control and access your data. For more information on these rights and how to exercise them, visit https://corporate.harlequin.com/california-privacy.

If offer card is missing write to: Harlequin Reader Service, P.O. Box 1341, Buffalo, NY 14240-8531 or visit www.ReaderService.com

BUSINESS REPLY MAIL
FIRST-CLASS MAIL   PERMIT NO. 717   BUFFALO, NY

POSTAGE WILL BE PAID BY ADDRESSEE

HARLEQUIN READER SERVICE
PO BOX 1341
BUFFALO NY 14240-8571

NO POSTAGE
NECESSARY
IF MAILED
IN THE
UNITED STATES

lukewarm water from the tap and mixed it with a few ounces of formula. He must have been thirsty because he guzzled it down in minutes. Then, right on cue, he burped and went to the bathroom. So now he's one happy camper, wrapped back up in a blanket, with a new diaper and a onesie to keep him dry."

Abby was smiling, though it was hard to take her seriously in her oversize hooded sweatshirt with the One Duck Shop logo across the front and the blue-and-gold-striped socks she must have found while searching in the store. But despite her oddly matched gear, she looked quite stylish. Her hair, still wet from their trek through the snow, seemed to shine even darker under the glow of the flashlight.

She looked down at the baby in her arms, her whole face wreathed in a huge grin. "I'm so glad that we could get this little guy out of the cold. He seems so much happier now, and he's finally gotten some color back in his cheeks. I know that Ricky and the others could head back to look for the baby. But it would be great if we could stay here long enough for him to warm up. I guess I wouldn't mind that, either."

"Me, too," he said. At least that was what he thought he said. His words seemed to have become jumbled in a whirlwind of feelings he hadn't experienced in a long, long time. He thought about the conversation they had had while making their way through the forest. Abby had opened up and shared the story of the accident that led to her decision to become a paramedic. Hearing her talk about her father's death gave him insight into the raw emotion he had seen in her eyes that day he had watched her at the scene of the car crash. The dedication she had shown in attempting to resuscitate that injured driver wasn't born out of competitiveness or a desire for glory. It was something baked hard into her DNA. And it was that same dedication powering her resolve to save the tiny infant left in her care.

"We can hole up here for a little bit longer," he said at last. "But we have to remember that we're still not safe. It's tempting to imagine that our pursuers have chosen to give up the chase. But it doesn't seem likely. Ricky won't rest until he gets his hands on his son."

Abby's smile faded. "We can't allow that to happen, Cal. We can't let those thugs kidnap the baby. I told Isobel I'd take care of him. I can't let her down."

He opened his mouth to respond and then closed it. How could he make Abby understand that nothing that had happened in the past few hours was her fault? He wanted to tell her that she was an amazing person— brave and strong and resourceful. That he had no doubt she'd be a wonderful mom to Davey, that she didn't have to prove herself to anyone, anymore.

Was this a good time for one of his stories? Interpersonal skills were not his strong suit, as Shannon had told him more than once. But that book of short biographies sure did come in handy at times like this. Each chapter in that little book had taught him that there were things about men and women—famous and ordinary—those around them often didn't see.

"What do you know about Faith Hill?" he asked.

"Who?" Abby looked up at him and frowned.

"Faith Hill. What do you know?"

"She's an extremely successful singer. And she's married to Tim McGraw. That's about it."

"All true. But were you aware that she once auditioned to become a backup singer for Reba McEntire, but she didn't get the job?"

"No, Cal, I did not know that. But I'm beginning to suspect that this is going to lead to another one of your inspirational tales."

Trust Abby to have figured out his technique.

"What if I told you that Faith Hill grew up singing in churches? And at age nineteen, she formed her own band that played at local rodeos. She even performed in a prison near her small town. She had talent, and she was determined to make a name for herself. All she needed was a chance."

Abby nodded. "So the moral here is that we need to harness that kind of determination when faced with problems up ahead."

Well, that was one way of looking at it. "That's true. But there is something else, too. Everyone knows that Faith Hill won a ton of music awards and had a lot of hit songs. But few people realize that she was adopted as an infant and raised by a couple who already had two biological sons of their own."

Abby's eyes flickered as she met and held his stare. "I get it, Cal. And thanks for the words of encouragement. I hope I can make that kind of difference in Davey's life, too."

Cal stroked his chin. "Exactly. As an adopted kid, I

am in a good position to say that what you're planning to do is terrific and brave. And you've done everything in your power tonight to keep Isobel's baby safe, so you shouldn't feel discouraged in any way." He paused to take a long breath. "So, moving on to the second message of my story, maybe we need to be creative as we think about making a plan. At least for the moment, it makes sense for us to camp out here for a bit and let the little guy warm up. I've got the front door booby-trapped, and the window taped closed with a rudimentary alarm system in place."

"What about the snowmobile?"

"I'm still hoping that I can get it to work. Except now I've sealed us up tight inside the store. I hate to take anything apart just to get outside."

"Nope." Abby rubbed the baby's back. "There's a side door next to the storage room. It leads out to the back of the store."

How did Abby know this stuff? He shook his head. "You seem pretty familiar with the layout of this place."

"Yeah. I used to work here back when I was a kid."

"I thought your brother told me that you were a waitress when you were in high school."

"I was. Later. But I worked here when I was younger."

Younger? How old was Abby when she got her first job? He wondered if it would be impolite to ask.

"I'll show you how to get out of here without setting off one of the traps." Abby's voice broke into his thoughts.

"Yeah. Sure." He was still processing what she had just told him as he turned and followed her across the store. She stepped behind the cashier's booth, reached beneath the counter and pulled out a jangle of keys. Then she ducked back around and wove to the far corner of the shop. Sure enough, there was a side door. He hadn't noticed it since it was lined up next to a closet.

Abby selected one of the keys and inserted it into the lock. She turned the handle and the door opened.

"Talk about a creative solution. This is great." A gust of wind lashed against his face as he propped his foot against the open door. "Any chance there's something on that key ring that might fit the snowmobile?"

Abby looked down and studied the keys. "I don't think so. They seem to be the wrong size to fit an ignition."

"I'll take them anyway. If I get the snowmobile going, I'll come back inside and let you know."

"Okay." Abby nodded. "In the meantime, I'll rig up some sort of sling so I can keep the baby with me while I move around the store. I'll put a couple of extra diapers and a bottle in the basket by the back door. And I suppose we should be thinking about rustling up some sort of dinner…or breakfast, I guess."

"Cereal's fine, and a couple of apples." He offered her a wide grin. "Not that I'd complain if all we snagged were some chips and chocolate candy. We can grab something to eat and plan our next move as soon as I come back inside."

He took the keys from Abby and gave a quick salute before heading toward the back of the store.

"Oh, and Cal." At the sound of Abby's voice, he swiveled back around to face her. "After I find some food, our little friend and I are going to hang out by the register. There's a video feed under the counter, and I'll be able to watch the front door and keep an eye out just in case the kidnappers return."

"Sounds good. I hope and pray that we've seen the last of Ricky, Max and Martina. At least until we face them in court." He turned and walked toward the side entrance.

A high drift was blocking the door, but he managed to shove it aside to create an opening wide enough for him to get through. The storm seemed to be letting up, and he was grateful for the increased visibility as he hurried toward the back of the building where the snowmobile was parked. But as he traced the beam of his flashlight across the vehicle's frame, his heart plummeted in his chest.

The snowmobile was older and more decrepit than he first realized, with a belly caked in dirt and rust, and a windshield cracked in two places. But the skis seemed intact, so once it got going, it would be a decent ride.

He straddled the seat and tried the keys in the ignition. None of them worked.

He moved to the front of snowmobile and reached under the hood. The latch popped open with a click. With his flashlight trained forward, he located the ignition and pulled out a tangle of wires.

He fiddled with them for a few minutes and then closed the hood. Maybe—just maybe—he might have done enough to make this thing work. He gripped the pull starter and was about to give it a yank when he detected the purr of an approaching vehicle. He flicked his flashlight off and, with his head bent low, moved toward the front of the store.

He waited a few seconds, and then he saw it—a dark SUV with its headlights off approaching from the other side of the road.

NINE

Abby sat beneath the service counter, her legs criss-crossed and her back pressed against the wall. It felt good to be still, holding a tiny infant in the makeshift sling close to her heart. She rolled her head back around on her neck and stretched her left arm across her chest. After the long trek through the snow, her body was feeling the strain and tensing up. She'd probably wake up with sore arms and legs in the morning. The morning? When was that? She glanced at the clock on the screen in front of her. 1:47. Even in the dark months of winter, daybreak was less than five hours away.

She glanced toward the back of the store, wondering if Cal was having problems with the snowmobile. At the thought of his clenched fingers fumbling with wires under a cold hood, a rush of guilt crowded her brain. It didn't seem fair that he was outside freezing while she was so warm and cozy inside the store. She had gathered up a couple of boxes of breakfast bars and a bunch of bananas that would serve as their breakfast when he returned. She hadn't been able to find any apples, but what was the other thing Cal had requested? Chocolate bars? She reached up and grabbed a couple extra-large packages of peanut butter cups from the display next to the counter to add to her stockpile.

Settling back into position, she scanned the two top screens of the video feed which showed the dark outline of the front door and the deserted pumps at the "easy-on, easy-off" ramp next to the road. A chill of apprehension shot down her spine as she thought about Isobel's husband, Ricky. Cal was right about Ricky not being the type of person to give up easily. Even though the SUV had driven past One Duck Shop without stopping, who was to say that it wouldn't be back? If Ricky was half as cunning as Isobel claimed, the discovery of their hiding place was inevitable.

She glanced at the lower screens on the shelf, which offered a bird's-eye view of the inside of the store. Mr. Ratten had set up monitoring devices at four surveillance locations. The extra precautions hadn't been necessary back when she had worked the register. But five years ago, there had been a number of incidents involving petty theft and vandalism. The crime wave continued for several weeks, and the police had been stymied in their attempts to catch the delinquents. Nearly a month had passed before three teenagers were apprehended when information was provided through an anonymous tip. A few weeks later, when she was picking up a coffee at One Duck Shop, Mr. Ratten had confided his secret. He had caught the culprits in action on his newly installed security cameras and revealed their identities to the police.

What would Mr. Ratten say when he arrived in the morning and discovered the broken window and watched the security tape of what had transpired overnight at the store? She'd been mentally keeping track of all of their "purchases" and had scrawled a quick note to explain. But Mr. Ratten wouldn't be worried about the lost revenue. He'd be glad to have done his part in protecting the town's citizens from the kidnappers.

She looked down at the baby. His eyes were closed, his lips pursed as he slept. How incredible that such a tiny human being was so tough and resilient. God was good. She closed her eyes and offered up a prayer of gratitude.

Bam.

Abby's eyes blinked open. Her gaze fixed on the top right video from the camera at the front of the building. It showed a shadowy figure pointing a shotgun at a blown lock on the door. The man—now clearly visible as Ricky—moved to the side of the threshold to allow his companion to enter before him.

Thunk.

"Ouch."

"What the…?"

At least Cal's makeshift booby trap seemed to have worked. Abby peered at the grainy images on the black-and-white screen. She still couldn't discern exactly what was happening. But judging from the shape of the silhouettes, the trip wire had sent Martina tumbling to the floor. And it was Ricky who had stepped over her prone body and, with his hands outstretched, was moving catlike along the wall.

She needed to get out of here—and fast. But before she could make a move, the lights blinked on, and the store was illuminated in a dull, yellow glow.

Uh-oh. From her current position, she could watch Ricky and Martina on the security cameras. But she would be a sitting duck as soon as they began to search the store. And where was Max? If he'd been tasked with checking the outside of the building, it would only be a matter of time before he came face-to-face with Cal.

It wouldn't be a fair fight. Max had a gun. And Cal was unarmed.

Ricky and his companions had already proven that anything that happened to her and Cal would be collateral damage to their plan to kidnap the baby. Abby's eyes flicked back to the security feed. Could she make it out the side door without being seen?

She glanced again at the screen. Ricky was halfway down an aisle on the left side of the store. And Martina was headed toward the back.

A torrent of expletives exploded into the air as the video feed clicked off and the store was plunged back into darkness. Abby felt her lips twitch into a smile. It appeared that Cal was alive and well, and doing everything he could to thwart the kidnappers. Including hitting the circuit breaker to kill the lights.

This was her chance. She needed to find a way to escape with the baby before Ricky realized what was going on. But even if she made it through the back door, where would she go and what would she do then? The best move she could make at the moment would be to try to take out Martina. It would be fitting after what happened in the parking lot at the bank.

Tucking the flashlight into her pocket, she pulled up the hood on her One Duck Shop sweatshirt and inched out from behind the counter, one hand cupped around the baby in the sling. "Sleep soundly, little one," she whispered, bending to kiss the infant's soft downy head. She moved slowly toward the back of the store, pausing as she passed the hardware section to let her fingers skim past the packets of picture hangers, nails and screws until they closed around a Phillips-head screwdriver.

Creak. Slam. Creak. Slam. From the sound of it, Martina was inside the bathroom, checking out the stalls. Abby made her way up the center aisle that led to the back of the store. As she turned the corner, she could see Martina exiting the restroom door and moving toward the janitorial closet. Although there was a hasp on the top edge of the door, the space was usually left unlocked, and Martina had no trouble twisting the handle and stepping inside.

Abby took a deep breath to calm her thundering heart. She knew what she needed to do. She rushed forward and slammed the door shut, moving quickly to flip the hasp and slide the screwdriver through the slot of the hinged metal plate. From inside the closet came a yelp of surprise, followed by the rat-a-tat of fists banging against the wood.

A sigh of relief passed through Abby's lips. Martina was trapped in the closet, at least for the time being. But Ricky was still on the prowl. Pressing her hand gently against the baby in the sling, she raced back down the aisle, stopping only to listen. Was that the soft tread of footsteps? They were close, and getting closer.

Should she make a run for it? As she looked down at the baby, two inky blue eyes blinked open with surprise. Pinpricks of anxiety twisted around her spine. *Please, Lord, don't let the little guy start to cry!* Even the smallest whimper would alert Ricky of his son's presence.

With silent steps, she crept forward, her ears straining for any indication that someone was nearby. She no longer heard footsteps. Had Ricky realized that she was getting closer? Goose bumps edged down her arm. She knew every nook and cranny of the space. She had the advantage. So why did it feel like she was the one being hunted?

She reached forward and felt the shelf on the left side of the aisle, letting her hand skim across hair accessories that were part of a bigger display. She picked up a hairbrush and flung it in the air. It clattered to the floor about twenty feet from the spot where she was standing. She paused and waited. There it was again, the soft tread of footsteps, moving in the opposite direction.

If she could sneak up on Ricky, she might be able to hit him over the head with her Maglite. But she'd need both hands to bring it down with the force needed to knock him out.

The movement stilled. Reluctantly, she lifted the baby from the sling and set him down in the basket by the door.

"I'll be right back," she whispered as she pulled the blanket around his tiny shoulders.

Gripping a flashlight in her hands, Abby turned and

waited. If she judged correctly, Ricky was in the next aisle over, just a short distance ahead of her. Hardly daring to breathe, she glanced to the left when she instantly realized her mistake.

"Gotcha!" A cruel voice whispered from the aisle to the right.

She froze midstep.

Ricky pulled her sideways, struggling to turn her around to face him. But as she raised her arm, her fingers clicked on the beam. Blinded by the light, Ricky loosened his grip, staggered backward and tumbled into a stack of cans.

Abby took off running. Behind her, she could hear the sound of her pursuer clamoring to his feet. She quickened her pace. *Faster. Faster.* Just a few more inches, and she'd be at the side door.

But as she reached out to grab the basket from the spot where she had set it, her heart sank in her chest.

The basket and the baby were gone.

Her eyes darted to the left and the right. Maybe this had been the plan all along. Maybe Ricky had been playing with her, letting her stalk him through the store while Max grabbed the baby. Anger and frustration coursed through her veins. It wasn't going to end like this. She turned her body, preparing for round two, when the side door clanked open and a long arm shot forward and snaked around her waist.

And with a hard tug pulled her through the door.

* * *

Cal waited until they were safely across the threshold before he released his grip on Abby's waist.

She stared at him, barely focusing, her eyes wild and her forehead pleated with confusion. But there wasn't time for explanations. Any second now, Ricky could come bursting through the door. Cal selected a thick branch from the woodpile and wedged it through the handle. It wouldn't buy them more than a few seconds, but that might be all they needed.

"C'mon," he whispered.

"No." Abby grabbed at his arm and gestured back toward the store. "We can't leave the baby."

"I've got him." Cal's voice was low and insistent.

"What?"

"I've got him!" He pointed toward the basket lodged against the front seat of the snowmobile. She rushed forward and scooped the infant into her arms. She slipped him back into the sling across her body, her face awash with relief. Her eyes blazed with a sudden fierceness as she scooted across the seat of the snowmobile.

He climbed up next to her and yanked the starter. The engine rumbled.

"Hold tight!" he shouted as he pulled on the throttle and pressed down on the accelerator. The vehicle lurched forward, and he could feel Abby shift backward from the sudden spurt of speed. He eased off the gas. The last thing he wanted was for his passengers to tumble off the back. A moment later, he felt her left arm twine around his waist and the pressure of a small body against his back. The baby was sandwiched between them, but there didn't seem to be any other configuration that would work.

Thud! The branch gave way, and the back door

crashed open. A shower of bullets rained through the air. Whoever was firing at them was clearly trying to disable their vehicle without harming the baby.

Cal slammed down on the accelerator.

"Stay low!"

He could feel Abby huddle down on her seat to protect the child between them.

He twisted on the handlebars, making the vehicle zig to the right and then to the left. The skis of the snowmobile sunk deeper to the ground, their speed drifting slower and slower as the vehicle fought against heavy drifts. Bits of ice and sleet bit at his face as he continued weaving from side to side.

They were almost to the road. A dusting of light flakes sparkled in the clear air, and a full moon illuminated the frozen landscape. He hunched his body lower. The rumble and the shouts suddenly seemed far away.

Ding!

A bullet grazed the side of the snowmobile. The vehicle tilted to the right, and the ski on the left side rose up out of the deep snow. Tipped on one side, the snowmobile actually seemed to be gaining momentum. Bracing his knees against the seat, Cal stood up and shifted his body to the left.

Thunk.

Another bullet missed its mark as the snowmobile settled back down on both skis. He turned and looked behind him.

"You okay?" he shouted to Abby.

Her head bobbed up and down against his back. He

glanced down. The bullet had scraped the side of the frame, but that seemed to be the extent of the damage.

As the snowmobile bumped down to the road, the skis slid easily along the more densely packed snow, and they began to pick up speed. This was more like it. Cal settled back against the seat. It felt like they were flying along the tarmac.

They were going to get out of this yet.

Crack. Still another bullet splintered the air.

But this one didn't miss.

It blazed through his skin and exploded into his leg.

TEN

The pain was excruciating. Hot and cold at the same time, like a burning, freezing hole in his calf sending sparks of agony up and down his leg. Ideally, Cal would take a few seconds to regain some control, but he couldn't take his eyes off the road. There were trees on one side and a ditch on the other, and he needed his wits about him if he was going to navigate through the deep drifts without veering off the edge of the road. He sucked air in through his nose and breathed it out with a gasp. His muscles tightened up, trying to ward off the throbbing torment from the wound. A sheen of sweat started at his neck and moved down to his toes as a cold clamminess settled over him. The hairs up and down his limbs were standing on edge. He shivered, trying to shake off the icy tremors seizing his body.

He drew in another breath. Slow and deep. The trauma from the gunshot was forcing his body to go into shock, but he couldn't allow that. It was crucial that he slow down his heartbeat and stay calm. Behind him, he could feel the warmth of Abby and the baby and the steady rhythm of their breathing. Relief and gratitude burst in his chest. At least they were okay.

Actually, all things considered, the escape from the convenience store had gone as well as he could have hoped. The old, run-down snowmobile was holding its own in the deep snow. And a bullet wound to the leg wasn't so bad. At least, he hadn't been hit in a vital organ.

For a moment there, when the black SUV had pulled into the driveway, it seemed as if all might be lost. The kidnappers' goal hadn't wavered from the beginning. They wanted the child, and they were prepared to take out anyone standing in their way.

Which meant him—and Abby. But that wasn't happening, at least not under his watch.

Priority one had been switching off the power. And once the lights were out, he was able to slip through the side door and grab the baby. Thankfully, the little guy was still asleep, so he'd placed the basket securely on the snowmobile and adjusted the blankets to ensure that he was settled down and warm in his nest. Then, he'd made a beeline back to the store to get Abby.

He had just pulled open the side door when she appeared, her eyes wide with panic. He didn't even have to think twice. He'd shot out his arm and pulled her across the threshold. After that—well, he was just glad that the engine of the snowmobile didn't stall out when he pulled the starter. And just like that they were on their way.

Thump.

The snowmobile thudded over a rock on the side of the road. How had they drifted all the way over to the shoulder? Cal blinked as he leveled the handlebars and directed the vehicle back in his lane. His brain felt fuzzy and sluggish. He seemed to have lost consciousness for a second there. Well, that was the wake-up call he needed. They were only four miles from town. Soon, they'd start to see houses and stores and other signs of civilization. All he had to do was to keep alert for fifteen more minutes.

Vrrrrooommmm. Vrrrrroooommmm. The growl of a vehicle approaching at top speed rumbled behind him.

"They're in their car, and they're following us!" Abby shouted over the wind.

There was a crack, and then a bullet whizzed by on the left.

"Hang on!" He pulled hard on the handlebars, steering the vehicle to the far side of the road. But the Land Rover followed his move and bumped up behind them. There was no way that the snowmobile was winning a race into town. He needed to do something. Fast.

He tightened his grip and yanked to the right. The snowmobile careened sideways and bounced down the embankment. The gully was just wide enough to accommodate the width of the skis. *Crack.* Another bullet zinged past. He pulled his gaze upward. The SUV loomed above them on the road.

Ricky leaned out the front window, a pistol in his hand.

Cal blew out a long sigh. His evasive strategy didn't seem to be working. He needed to get out of the ditch onto more open space where the snowmobile would have the advantage.

His brain seized upon an idea. The lake!

A whisper of apprehension niggled at his mind. Winter this year had been relatively mild. There had been plenty of snow, but the temperatures hadn't dipped too often into the single digits. The ice was thick enough to support a light structure and a couple of ice fishermen. It might even be strong enough to hold a snowmobile with two riders. But for larger vehicles, the ice wasn't safe. Just last week, he had answered a 911 call from a couple of teenagers in a Jeep who had decided to take a shortcut across the lake. Right when they reached the middle, where the ice was its thinnest, the surface had cracked and their vehicle began to sink. His team had rescued them before they went under, but the accident served as a dire reminder of the dangers of driving on the lake. Could he risk taking Abby and the baby out there?

Another bullet zinged by, and he made up his mind.

He had to take that risk. It was their only option. Yes, the ice was thin, but the snowmobile was lighter than a car, and he could stick close to the shore where the frozen surface was thicker and more secure. Up ahead was his chance. A service road intersected the highway. He hunched his body lower. Ten more feet. Five. Wrenching the handlebars to the right, he stomped on the accelerator, and the snowmobile pivoted sideways, whizzing out of the ditch. With a jarring thump, they landed hard on the snow-covered pavement.

Behind them came the screech of tires as the SUV driver slammed on the brakes. But Cal had been expecting that. He veered off the tarmac and plunged down the incline toward the lake.

The handlebars jiggled in his hands as the snow-mobile picked up speed on the icy slope. His knuckles were white, but he held steady as Abby's arms stiffened against his waist. She had to know that they were on the very edge of losing control. All it would take would be one rock on the path, one heavy branch jutting out of the snow, and the nose of the snowmobile would tip forward and hurl all of them into the air.

The drop-off was just in front of them. Cal tensed as they jumped the embankment and thudded down hard onto the lake.

There was an ominous clunk as they nailed the landing. Beneath the skis, the ice groaned. The engine sputtered, coughed and then chugged back to life. And on a wing and a prayer, they were back on their way.

Thunk! Vibrations rippled across the surface as the SUV dropped onto the ice behind them and took chase. The roar of its engine hummed in the air.

Cal veered away from the shoreline and aimed for the center of the lake.

The SUV raced to overtake them.

Cal gunned the motor, leaning in hard to gain an advantage over the much faster vehicle. But the Land Rover closed the gap in record time. It was less than five feet away from them when a deep rumble ruptured the air.

Wooosh. Crrraaaacccckkk.

Cal held his breath as the ice began to splinter on either side of him.

* * *

Abby hung on for dear life as prickles of fear danced up and down her spine. How could this be happening? Didn't Cal know that the ice was too thin to withstand their weight? Details from the accident last week played across her mind. Those teenagers had been fortunate. Fifteen minutes longer, and hypothermia would have set in. Cal had been there, along with other members of the rescue team. He knew what happened. So, what was he thinking?

And Abby herself was well-versed on the dangers of driving across the lake. At least three or four foolhardy individuals died each year when the vehicle they were driving crashed through the ice. It had happened to a boy in her class during senior year. And as a paramedic, she always dreaded the calls to the lake, winter or summer. Drowning seemed like such a senseless way to die. And drowning under a twelve-inch barrier of ice was even worse.

She closed her eyes and prayed.

The roar of the ice breaking up beneath them assailed her ears. Any minute now, the snowmobile might plunge into the frozen waters. She looked down at the baby in her arms. *Please, God, protect him and keep him from harm.*

Crash! Splash! Was it happening? She opened her eyes. Cal was still at the controls, but the snowmobile was edging back toward the shore. She turned around just in time to see the front of the SUV slip slowly through the surface of the lake.

"We don't have enough fuel to get us back to town.

I'm going to head toward the Red Fox Lodge!" Cal shouted over the din. "Maybe there's someone there with a cell phone."

They could only hope. But given the storm and the treacherous driving conditions, it was unlikely that any staff would be around to help. The place was closed between December and March, except for the occasional handyman making repairs. It was a different story in the summer months when visitors flocked to the resort from the cities to hike the trails, canoe and kayak on the lake. There were a number of small cabins for families and a main lodge that served meals. Nothing fancy, just good home cooking. And a chance to escape the stress of city life.

Abby shifted in her seat. A strange wetness was seeping through her pant leg, distracting her thoughts. Her entire body was cold and damp from the flying snow. But why did one spot feel so much wetter than the rest?

She looked down at the baby. He stared back at her with huge blue eyes, almost as if he sensed her accusation. But there was no way that his diaper could have soaked through to her leg. And it was spreading. Now the entire bottom edge of her pants felt sodden and damp.

Uh-oh. Was there a leak in one of the tanks on the snowmobile? With all of the bullets flying through the air, it was more than possible that something had been hit. Maybe the wetness was oil or gas.

"Cal?" she yelled.

No answer.

The snowmobile was still moving forward, but Cal's driving had become erratic, almost jerky as he edged from side to side. Maybe they were running out of gas. Or maybe Cal was trying to make their tracks less obvious to anyone following their trail.

Would Ricky and the others come looking for them? Probably. The question was when. It would take a while for the SUV to sink, and it was likely that the three kidnappers would escape before their vehicle sunk through the ice. But it was impossible to predict what the kidnappers would do next. They'd be wet and cold and in desperate need of dry clothing. They might head back to the road and attempt to commandeer a passing vehicle. Or hole up at the convenience store to find some warm gear.

In either case, it would be at least a half-mile trek before they reached their destination. Whatever Ricky, Max and Martina decided to do, it would be hours before they would be ready to resume the chase.

Meanwhile, she and Cal would have some precious time to regroup and make a plan to get away, Even if they couldn't locate a cell phone, there was a Quonset hut somewhere behind the lodge where management stored ATVs, paddle boats and other equipment. It might be a bumpy ride, but a hopped-up Gator could get them to town in thirty minutes or less. Abby's lips bent into a smile at the thought of reuniting Isobel with her son.

Just that quickly, her smile faded into a worried frown. Poor Iz. She must be worried sick, wondering what had happened to her little boy. But soon all those fears would be banished. Life as she knew it would return to normal. The kidnappers would be behind bars, and Isobel and her baby would be safe at last.

As Abby leaned sideways to see how far they still had to go, a gasp stuck in her throat. The snowmobile was no longer headed in a straight line toward the lodge. The shoreline curved around the bend toward a cluster of rocky inlets. And the snowmobile appeared to be on a collision course with one of the many stone outcroppings jutting out above the snowy drifts.

"Cal! Watch out! There are rocks up ahead," she cried.

"Sorry!" Cal's voice was soft. Almost slurry. But he yanked the handlebars to the left and made a quick correction. When Abby peered forward, she could see that the tips of the skis once more pointed in the right direction.

As they closed in on the shore, she could make out the first cabin beside the edge of the lake. Would Cal head straight for the main building? She wouldn't be sorry if he did. She hadn't had the time to retrieve the stockpile of food she had gathered at the convenience store, and her stomach had an empty, gnawing feel that wouldn't be sated by the one granola bar she had tucked into her back pocket. If all went well, they might be able to scrounge up something to eat in the lodge kitchen.

If they could make it to shore. The snowmobile had slowed down to a crawl as they bumped on to the snow-covered beach. She ought to be pleased, but the strange dampness she had noticed before was still seeping into the material covering her right leg. Releasing her grip around Cal's waist, she reached down and felt for the source of the wetness. There didn't seem to be anything leaking from the belly of the snowmobile. She touched her leg.

Her heart seemed to stop for half a second. The sticky substance pooled on her pants felt like blood.

"Cal!" she shouted.

"Almost there," he replied.

She looked down. Sure enough, her fingers were splattered with the dark red of a deep wound. She raised her arm and placed her other hand against Cal's head. It was damp and clammy with perspiration.

"Cal! You're going into shock. You need to pull over and let me drive. Now!"

"Almost there," he replied again. His head bobbled on his neck as the snowmobile sputtered past a sign welcoming them to Red Fox Lodge, weaved around a line of snowbanks left behind by the plow and chugged toward the entrance.

They had barely come to a stop when Abby slid off the back and ran toward the door. Clutching the baby against her chest, she jiggled the handle. The door creaked open. The last person to exit the lodge must not have taken the time to turn the latch, and it was a mistake for which she was grateful.

She couldn't stop and look around, even for a minute. She set the baby on the floor and sprinted back outside to find Cal with his eyes closed and his body slumped down on the seat of the snowmobile.

ELEVEN

"Cal! Cal!" Abby's breath came out in desperate gasps as she aimed the beam of her flashlight at Cal's leg. The material on the bottom half of his overalls was sodden with blood and caked over with ice, and there was a tear in the fabric where the bullet had ripped into his calf. The good news was that it looked like a clean shot through the muscle. The bad news was that he had lost a lot of blood. Too much.

"Cal." Abby reached out and touched his hand. "We need to get you inside."

His eyes were open now, but his body was beginning to tremble. He was going into shock. How had he managed to drive the snowmobile with such a deep wound in his leg? Between the loss of blood and pain, most people would have passed out. But Cal had to be running on adrenaline. Besides, he wasn't like most people. He was made of sterner stuff. A part of her wanted to yell at him and demand to know why he hadn't stopped earlier, but she already knew the answer. Ever the sheriff, he believed his first consideration was always for others, never himself. To serve and protect, no matter the cost.

Well, today the cost was steep. A critical injury that required immediate treatment. But it wouldn't cost him more than that. Not if she had her way.

She nudged his shoulder gently.

"Abby?" His eyelids fluttered. "How's the baby?"

Slurred speech. Not a good sign.

"The baby is fine. But I need to get you inside so I can patch up your leg." She spoke in a matter-of-fact voice, reverting to paramedic mode—cool, calm, steady, detached. The last bit would be the hardest. She could feel her heart thudding as the impossibility of the situation hit her. They were stranded on the far side of a partially frozen lake at a lodge that was closed for the season. And Cal had a gaping bullet hole in his leg. But no way was she giving up. Not now, after they had made it this far.

"Okay, but you need to park the snowmobile behind the lodge." Cal's words were barely coherent. "In case Ricky manages to find a way across the lake. Maybe if he doesn't see any activity, he won't realize we are here."

"I'll do that. But first, I'm going to help you scoot sideways so you can dismount," she explained. She walked around to the left side of the snowmobile and bent Cal's knee upward so that she could push it over the seat. She dashed back around to the spot where she had been standing and placed an arm around his waist. "On the count of three, I'm going to hold you steady while you push yourself up. One." She widened her stance and braced her body. "Two... Three."

She pulled upward, to provide support as Cal heaved

his body off the snowmobile. He stood still for a moment, swayed back and forth and then, with a grunt, took a step forward.

With her arms laced around Cal's waist, she led him into the lodge. Step. Lurch. Step. Lurch. Perspiration beaded on Abby's brow. Each step required a renewed mustering of strength to counter Cal's crushing weight. When they finally reached the large sofa in the middle of the floor, she took a deep breath. Her heart was pounding from the exertion, but she didn't have time to pause. Cal's face was ashen, and a deep crimson stain spread across his pant leg. Quickening her pace, she helped him lie down so she could complete the procedural ABCs—checking his airway, breathing and circulation. Good news. Although his breath was shallow and his pulse was faint, his heart was still beating with a steady rhythm.

Cal was a fighter.

But unless she was able to stop the bleeding, that wouldn't be enough.

She shook off her frustration and resolved to remain calm. This wouldn't be the first time she was forced to think on her feet, and it wouldn't be the last. She raised her head to scope out the space. The main lobby extended along the front of the building, with a check-in desk at the back and a smattering of upholstered couches and chairs set in front of the windows where guests could relax and enjoy the view. In her rush to return to help Cal disembark from the snowmobile, she had set the baby down inside on the floor, and, at least for the moment, the little guy had gone back to sleep.

And—excellent! There was a bathroom just around the corner from the main desk.

But first things first. She needed to do as Cal had asked and hide the snowmobile.

Five minutes later, she was back inside, yanking sheet after sheet of paper towels out of the dispenser. She grabbed the bottle of hand soap from the sink and raced back to the spot where she had left Cal on the couch.

Cal's overalls were shredded where the bullet had ripped through the leg, so she gripped the opening and gave a hard pull, splitting the fabric in two. A drop of perspiration trickled down her forehead as she reached for a stack of paper towels and set them in place against the gaping hole. But try as she might, she couldn't provide sufficient pressure to stop the flow of blood. What she needed was a tourniquet.

She drummed her fingers against her chin. She headed back toward the reception desk and began to open and close drawers. What she was looking for, she wasn't certain, but she'd know it when she found it. She grabbed a pile of napkins, a bottle of hand sanitizer, a box of plastic utensils and a miniature sewing kit with an assortment of needles stuck through a scrap of soft cotton fabric in the packet. What else did she need? The pickings were slim. Nothing useful caught her eye.

She ran back to Cal.

She set the items she had gathered on the floor, pulled off her sweatshirt and quickly unbuttoned her wool cardigan. The turtleneck she wore underneath didn't provide any warmth, but it would have to do for the moment. She looped her sweater's arms just above the bullet hole on Cal's leg and then ripped open the box of utensils and grabbed a handful. With a handful of plastic knives, she twisted the makeshift tourniquet tightly around the leg. It was primitive, and it wasn't pretty. But it was going to work.

As the blood slowed to a trickle, she headed back to the restroom and turned on the faucet. Reaching across the counter for more paper towels, she ripped off a handful and held them under the water until they became soggy. Then she ran back to Cal and began to clean off the blood so she could examine the wound.

It was deep, but the bullet had grazed the fleshy part of his leg and missed the bone. If she had the proper supplies, she could sew it up. Even duct tape would suffice as a temporary fix, but she hadn't found any in her search.

She had a needle, but she needed thread strong enough for the suture. The material in her parka wouldn't do, and neither would the canvas cloth of Cal's overalls. Her sweater? She picked at the seam but the delicate wool fabric frayed in her fingers.

There had to be something she had missed. She looked around, and right in front of her was the answer. Her bracelet. The one with the multicolored beads and the delicate laces tied at the sides. Laces that could be separated into strands thin and pliable as dental floss.

She cast a pained look at Cal. It was ironic that the person who had felt the need to comment on her fashionable clothing would now benefit from her choice of jewelry. Although the sheriff looked pale and drawn

in his unconscious state, she couldn't help but imagine
that he was smiling under his goatee. *We'll discuss this
later*, Cal, she thought as she reached for the pincush-
ion she had found in the desk. As a final precaution,
she washed everything with hand sanitizer, threaded
the needle and began the suture.

Cal's eyes blinked open, fluttering away the rainbow
of colors dancing inside of his head. Was he asleep? Had
he been dreaming?

He turned his head and looked down at the scatter-
ing of beads on the table next to the sofa—blue, green,
pink and pale yellow. Well, that explained the rainbow.
He flexed his arms and tried to push himself up, but his
body felt cemented in place.

"Lie still while I finish stitching your leg."

Abby stood above him, her eyes glinting as she tied
a string to the end of a needle. "Steady, now. This might
hurt."

That was putting it mildly.

He clenched his hands into fists as Abby bent forward and continued her work. Her features were a study
of concentration as she wove the needle in and out. Part
of him suspected that she was enjoying brandishing her
tiny weapon against his tender flesh.

He closed his eyes again as a wave of pain traveled
across his leg.

A fog of confusion addled his brain. The last thing
he remembered was Abby holding him steady as they
made their way through the front door of the lodge. She
had helped him get settled against the striped pillows of

the couch. And then—she must have somehow found a way to stop the bleeding in his leg.

It was nothing short of astonishing, especially since, for a while there, he'd thought he might die, stretched across the seat of a snowmobile, parked in front of Red Fox Lodge. His thoughts may have been muddled, but he knew that he wasn't ready to go out like that. He had too many things left on his bucket list. Like going trout fishing in Wyoming. Meeting his newest nephew. Reconnecting with his parents. Not that he was at odds with them. But their relationship had been strained since Shannon's death. For a long time, he felt dishonest discussing his marriage. His family wanted to push him into the role of grieving widower, and though it was true that he was mourning the loss of a person he'd once loved, only he knew that he and Shannon had plans to divorce.

As a result, he had avoided them more and more. Forgetting birthdays. Skipping Thanksgiving. Making only a token appearance at Christmas. In fact, if he wasn't rescuing a baby from a murderous band of thugs at this particular moment in time, he would probably be plotting his excuse for skedaddling out early from the fishing weekend with his dad.

But his parents deserved better. They had given him a family. Picked him out, when no one else wanted him. Raised him as their own. His dad always told him that it wasn't common blood that made a family. It was love. And he had been loved by them. It didn't matter that they didn't share the same DNA. He had always known that he was their true son.

But talk about a reality check. With life hanging in the balance, all his worries vanished like smoke in the wind. And right then, he promised himself that if he lived to see another day, he'd work harder to be a better son. A more effective sheriff. A kinder friend.

"All done." Abby's sensible voice interrupted his musings. "Now I am going to release the tourniquet. It might feel weird for a few seconds."

His mind registered her words, but they didn't add up until he felt a tingling and then a sudden rush of blood flow into his leg. For a moment, they both stared at the neat row of stiches, waiting to see if they would hold.

Abby smiled. "I think we're okay. You'll have to get this all redone at a hospital when we get back home." She paused and then added in a quiet voice, "If we get home."

"Oh, we're going to get home. In fact, I'll be ready to go in a minute."

Cal pulled himself up from the couch.

"Cal, no. You need to wait until you're strong enough to move around."

He shook off her caution and stepped gingerly down on his leg. Pain stabbed through his muscles as he stumbled forward, barely managing to avoid falling on to the floor. Panting from the exertion, he steadied himself against the coffee table, willing the ache to subside.

He looked down at the stiches. Abby had probably saved his life. He wasn't certain that there was another person, male or female, in all of Dagger Lake County, let alone the state of North Dakota, who would have been competent enough to create a suture under such dire circumstances. But why did the white string, woven in a neat row on the side of his leg, look so familiar? He knew that Abby had used a needle to stich up his leg. He had experienced the stabbing pain firsthand. But where had she found the thread? He had seen the pale lacing before, but couldn't place it.

He closed his eyes for just a moment and unclenched his fingers from the table's edge.

A throbbing pain shot up his side, practically paralyzing him with its intensity. Desperate for relief, he swayed, his knees buckling beneath him. Holding on to a chair, he lowered himself to the floor. The coolness of the tile soothed the burning ache, at least temporarily.

Abby reached down and touched his leg. "The stitches held. I think we're good. But honestly, Cal, I wasn't kidding when I said that you need to take it easy."

Inspiration dawned. "Hey. I just figured it out. I thought the thread you used on my leg looked familiar. It was from your bracelet. You took it apart. And pulled off the beads."

"So I did."

"Well, thanks for stitching me up, Doc." Cal pushed up to a sitting position and leaned against the back of the table for support.

"You're welcome. But don't try to stand again until I tell you it's okay." She pulled a granola bar out of her back pocket. "Maybe you can munch on this while we wait. Fifteen minutes of quiet is all I ask, and then we can see if you're feeling up to it."

"How about ten?" he bargained with a smile.

"Fine. But you need to give your body a chance to recover. It would be best if you stayed still for at least a half hour."

He unwrapped the bar and took a bite. He chewed thoughtfully, and then he shook his head. "That won't work. I need to be ready. Ricky and the others are still out there somewhere. But where they are at the moment, I just can't be sure."

"But they have to be wet and cold. And without a vehicle."

"Maybe. But after everything that has happened, I can't see them throwing in the towel and giving up."

He wanted to say more. But before he could speak, a serious wail echoed across the rafters.

The baby was awake. And from the sound of it, he wasn't happy.

TWELVE

Abby lifted the crying baby in her arms. Poor little guy. His face was the color of a red tomato, and his fingers were clenched into tiny fists. "I think he's hungry again, and probably wet, as well. Unfortunately, I put all the extra diapers and formula in his basket. And that got tossed when we made our escape."

"I jammed all of that under the seat before I set the basket on the snowmobile."

She handed him the baby. "Well done on that, Cal. While you hold our angry friend, I'll go retrieve our stash."

The supplies were just where Cal had said they would be. Once she was back inside, she made quick work of changing the baby's diaper. She thought the baby might need some more formula, but Cal immediately took the infant in his arms and began rocking him back to sleep.

"Why don't I take him and give you a break?" Abby said.

"Nah. I kind of like that cute way he snorts when he's starting to settle down. Like his caregivers finally got the message, and all's right with the world."

Abby looked away to hide her smile. This was a side of the gruff sheriff that she had seen more than once during the past hours they had spent together. He put on a good act, but underneath, he was a softy just like her.

"Yeah," Cal continued. "I've always liked kids. When I was married, I hoped that we'd have a couple of our own. There's something sort of awesome about watching them grow. Like everyday evidence of God's loving care. I remember holding my nephews and nieces when they were born and thinking about all the milestones that awaited them up ahead. Learning to walk and starting to talk. Grade school. High school. College. Setting out in the world and fulfilling their dreams." He chucked softly. "The time goes fast, and before you know it, they're getting married themselves."

Wow. In all the time she had known Cal, that was the longest she had ever heard him talk about something so personal. In truth, Cal had always been a bit of an enigma. Not exactly standoffish. Reserved seemed to be a more apt description. He maintained his distance and didn't share much about his past. And Abby respected that. After her dad died, she had shut down a lot of conversations by refusing to describe the details of the accident or to share what she had been feeling those last few moments the two of them had been stuck in the car. So she understood his need for playing it close to the chest. But now it seemed that Cal was making it clear that his private life was no longer off-limits and that he was willing to finally open up.

She knew a little bit about Cal's wife's death and his decision to move to Dagger Lake to make a new start. That part of his backstory had been grist for the gossip mill in the first few months after he arrived in town. But no one seemed to know exactly what transpired in the tragic, officer-involved shooting in Saint Cloud. There had been rumors that Cal's wife had not followed proper procedure in handling a domestic dispute, that she had ignored the rules and tried to diffuse a dangerous situation on her own. It would have been easy to find out most of the details, but Abby thought it was best not to pry.

Still, Cal was the one who had brought the subject of his marriage up, so it seemed safe to assume that he wanted to talk about it.

She took a deep breath. "Cal, I know your wife died in the line of duty. I can't even begin to imagine how hard that must have been for you. And I just want you to know that I am very sorry for your loss."

Cal nodded. "Thanks, Abby. What happened with Shannon is all part of the public record, so it's no big secret how it all went down."

"I don't really know any of the specifics. I figured it was none of my business."

"I appreciate that. The whole thing is still so difficult for me to understand. Shannon had just gone off duty when she got a call about a domestic dispute. Backup was less than two minutes away, but she decided not to wait. She rushed right in, determined to make an arrest. Turned out the husband of the woman who had called in the complaint had a big old rifle and an even bigger death wish going for him. Shannon never had a chance."

Abby blew out a long breath. "That's terrible. It sounds like she was very brave."

"She was. According to the incident report, she showed courage to the point of being foolhardy. And that last part of the equation ended up costing her life."

"Knowing that it might have gone down differently if she had waited for backup must have made the loss even harder for you."

"It did. But the truth is, Abby, even before the shooting, Shannon and I weren't on the same page about a lot of things. We met at the police academy and got married a month after graduation. And we started having problems immediately. We were too different, I guess. I believed in following rules, and she was a maverick, always wanting to be in the middle of all the action, even when it was the last place she belonged. We argued about it quite a bit, especially after she was written up for risking her partner's life in a drug bust downtown. When she agreed to go to marriage counseling, I thought the situation would to take a turn for the better, but that didn't end up being the case. During one of our sessions, the counselor asked about our ten-year plan for our lives. Mine was pretty typical—kids, a bigger house, a bigger yard, vacations with the family." He shrugged. "Shannon's plan didn't include kids—or me. It focused on a rise up the ranks, with her eventually becoming a captain of a large city police force. Needless to say, I felt blindsided."

Abby pressed her lips together. She didn't know what to say.

"Not surprisingly, we drifted apart. We called it a

trial separation, but we both knew that it was the first step in an inevitable move toward divorce. We were keeping the situation a secret from our colleagues at the station while we worked out the details, so when she died, everyone assumed that I was a grieving widower. It was true that I was grieving, but I felt like a fraud because no one knew that our marriage had been over for almost a year before she died.

"Sorry," he said. "That story is kind of a downer. Maybe I need to stick to things from my book of biographies. Let me think." He pressed his lips together and tilted to his head. "Okay. I got one. So, what do you know about…?"

Abby held up her hand. "How about *I* tell *you* a story for a change?"

He said, straightening his back against the pillow, "That would be better. I'm all ears."

"Okay. My story is about a woman named Miriam. You won't find her name or picture in any history books, but she made a big difference in the lives of the foster kids she took in and raised as her own. Her house was right next door to the place I lived with my mom and brother when we came to live on the reservation."

"That was after your dad died, right?"

"Yeah. My mom had been struggling even before we moved to Dagger Lake. But once we were surrounded by a network of family and friends, she took a major step backward on her parental responsibilities. Unfortunately, most of our relatives didn't realize how checked out my mom really was, especially when it came to us kids."

Abby was quiet for a moment as she thought about the night she had shown up in her brother's classroom to watch him perform in a school play. None of the other parents in attendance acted like anything was amiss about an eleven-year-old wearing a name tag that said "Mrs. Marshall." But several days later, there was a knock on the door of their house, and there was Miriam.

"But it all got better when Gideon and I began spending time after school with Miriam. She taught us so many practical things and quite a few life lessons, too. How to be strong and brave. How to climb off your high horse to lend a friend a helping hand. She was awesome. One of those adults that can relate to kids while still managing to be firm but fair. Miriam died a couple years ago, and over five hundred people came to her funeral. Five hundred. Can you believe it? One guy even flew in all the way from Australia. That's the kind of person she was."

She looked down and touched the hem of her blouse.

"She taught you to sew, didn't she?"

Abby nodded. "She did. She showed me how to make a pattern and then find the perfect fabric for just the right look. It was great when I was in high school because I had the skills to whip up a new outfit in just a couple of hours."

"Well." He took a deep breath as he once again trained his gaze on the baby in his arms. "You always look very nice, so I'm guessing that you must be an excellent seamstress."

She smiled. "Thanks, Cal."

He shook his head. "We both have quite the sad sto-

ries to share, don't we? But think about this. Thanks to
our combined forces, we've been able to give this little
guy a chance at a happy ending. Because if we hadn't
arrived on the steps of the bank when we did, his mom
would be dead, and he would have been kidnapped by
his dad. And no one would be the wiser." Cal looked
down at the baby in his arms.

Then he lowered his lips and kissed the little boy's
head.

Abby had started to cry, and Cal wasn't sure why.
He thought that his comment about them saving the
baby would make her happy. Then again, maybe she
was happy. He detected the trace of a smile through
her tears.

"Thanks for listening to my tale of woe," he said.

Abby shot him a bemused look.

He hastened to explain. "About Shannon and everything. I never told anyone—not even my parents—that
Shannon and I were separated and living apart at the
time she got shot. I guess I thought that it would only
disappoint them. And since she was gone, it didn't seem
necessary. But it felt good to share the story with you
and allow the truth to be out in the open."

Abby pushed back her tears. "I know I said it before,
but I'm really glad we decided to be friends."

He was, too. Even though he had plenty of acquaintances—Abby's brother Gideon, a few of the reg-
ulars who met every day at the diner for breakfast—he
didn't have many true friends. He wasn't a guarded
person by nature, but Shannon's death had caused him

to become closed off and cautious in his personal interactions. And it didn't help that he was the sheriff. People loved to buttonhole him when he was out and about, offering up helpful suggestions and advice. But for all their talk, conversations never went beyond the superficial.

Not Abby though. With her, he felt comfortable sharing his deeper feelings and letting her see who he was beyond the uniform and the job.

The sudden clatter of something crashing into a window claimed his attention. A gnarled branch pressing against the glass and rattling in the wind. A sigh of relief left his lips. Nothing to worry about this time. But Ricky and the others were out there somewhere, waiting to strike. The lodge might be warm and comfortable, but it was far from safe.

Abby had to know that, too. She had stopped crying, but she was still upset. It had been an arduous couple of hours, filled with close calls and last-minute escapes. Of course, she was worried. She had been thrust into the role of midwife and protector of the newborn who had been left in her care. In fulfilling her promise to Isobel, Abby would do whatever it took, even if it meant putting her own life and dreams on the line.

Dreams like adopting Davey Lightfoot. He remembered the kid well. A solemn little boy who had been dealt a tough hand in life. He should have been surprised by Abby's intention to make a home for the child. She had always seemed so dedicated to her career, always ready to work extra shifts, not seeming to have much of a life beyond her paramedic work. But it made sense when he thought about it. Over the past few hours, he had seen firsthand how selfless she was. Turned out he had been right about some of the details, but wrong about almost everything else. In fact, he was wrong about so many things related to Abby Marshall that it made his head spin just thinking about it. He didn't want to stop and consider why this new information filled him with excitement and warmth. It was enough that it did.

Telling Abby about Shannon's death had helped him understand something surprising about himself. The comparisons he had been making between Abby and Shannon? They didn't add up. Maybe focusing on a bunch of superficial similarities was just his way of protecting his heart.

"Why don't I take the baby and give you a break?" Abby stretched out her arms. For a moment, she held the little boy close, and then she slipped him back into the sling around her chest. "Time for a nap, little friend," she said, tucking in the sides of the blanket and running her fingers over his soft tufts of hair.

She walked over and sat down on the couch, her forehead wrinkled as she turned toward him with a worried smile.

"I know you're right about Ricky. After everything that has happened, we shouldn't allow ourselves to assume we're safe. I'm not as familiar with this place as I was with the convenience store. But my brother worked here one summer when he was in high school, and I remember him saying that there's a hut where they keep the golf carts and ATVs behind the main premises. There's a chance that the keys to all the vehicles are hanging inside on a board. So you might not need to use your skill set for hot-wiring ignitions."

"Hey! My talents came in handy with the snowmobile. But checking out the ATVs is a good idea. It would be smart to find some potential transportation out of here just in case our friends show up."

"You're a man of many talents, Sheriff Stanek. But—" her forehead creased as she looked down at his leg "—your stitches aren't really looking all that good. I think the baby and I should wander into the kitchen to see if we can find something nourishing for you to eat."

"Sounds like a plan. But I'm coming with you. My leg has started to stiffen up from lack of movement."

Abby seemed to consider this for a couple of seconds before offering him her hand. "Okay. We can go together. Check the place out. Let me know if you start to feel woozy. We can always stop and rest."

It felt nice to hold on to Abby's arm as they shuffled past the circular staircase in the main reception area and the small gift shop that sold baseball caps and T-shirts emblazoned with the lodge's red fox logo. And his closeness to Abby gave him a bird's-eye view of the baby, sound asleep in the sling across her chest.

He stumbled twice. Abby tightened her grip to steady his gait. Once inside the paneled dining room, they made their way across the carpeted floor. It was a large space, but the tables and chairs stacked around the edges made it seem more like a ballroom than a dining facility. Along the back wall, there was a long table, covered end-to-end with jumbo-size warmers and empty trays.

Cal tried to imagine the selection at the breakfast buffet. Scrambled eggs and pancakes. Omelets cooked to order with peppers and cheese. A dessert section laden with cinnamon buns and glazed doughnuts.

His stomach growled at the prospect.

Once they passed through the swinging doors to the kitchen, Cal let go of Abby's arm and braced himself against the stainless steel workspace used to prepare meals for lunch and dinner. He edged along past the pots and pans hanging from racks on the ceiling toward a small refrigerator on the far side of the kitchen.

He took a deep breath and released his grip on the counter. He had made it this far with Abby's help, but it was time to put pressure on his leg. "From here on in, I'll try to do this on my own."

"Hmm. Just take it slow and easy. And remember that I'm here if you want to stop and catch your breath. Let's see what we can find in the fridge. Maybe the custodian left behind a couple sandwiches before he left for home."

A guy could hope. The positive effects of that granola bar had long worn off. But nope, the only edible item in the unit was a package of English muffins crumbling at the edges.

Abby slipped it into the plastic bag that had been left on the counter. From the open shelves next to the freezer, she grabbed a butter knife, a jar of strawberry jam and a gift-wrapped block of cheese still in its packaging and stuffed everything into the sack. "Beggars can't be choosers, right? Let's take all this back to the reception area. That way, we can keep an eye on what's happening outside and feast while we discuss our next move."

Feast? Not likely. But this was probably the best of their limited options. He reached across the workspace for one of the large knives hanging next to a prep station. "I'll take this just in case we need it to slice the cheese."

By the look in her eyes, she knew what he was thinking—that a sharp weapon might prove useful if Ricky and the others showed up.

The trek back to the reception area was twice as grueling without the support of Abby's arm. His heart raced, and his muscles throbbed with exhaustion. But he gritted his teeth and maintained a steady pace.

Abby helped him get settled on the couch and then knelt down on the floor. With a colorful throw she found slung across one of the chairs, she made a bed next to the couch and then gently eased the baby out of the sling and onto the blanket she had placed on the floor. Then, pushing aside the ripped fabric on Cal's pants, she bent over to check his leg. "There's still some leaking in the area around the stitches. You can rest while you get something to eat."

She splashed a squirt of sanitizer on her hands. Once her hands were clean, she spread out the items she had gathered for their dinner. She split open the muffins and smeared them with jam. Though he had been daydreaming about pancakes dripping with butter and syrup, the muffins tasted mighty good, and a second helping went a long way toward relieving his hunger pains.

Abby ate quickly and then pushed herself up and

headed toward the reception desk. "I was thinking that there must be a map of this place around somewhere." Her head disappeared under the counter. She reappeared seconds later with a brochure in her hand. "Here we go." She walked over to the couch and unfolded the leaflet on the table. She pointed to a semicircular building on the far side of the map. "This is the hut I was telling you about where they keep the ATVs. But it looks pretty far from the main lodge. It's way past the cabins in the back of the lot."

"I think I can make it."

Abby seemed doubtful. "I'm not sure about that. But check out what I found in one of the drawers." She reached in her pocket and pulled out a lanyard clip with one large key. "It's labeled 'Vehicle hut.' So getting in should be a piece of cake." She paused, then shook her head. "Wow…um… I just thought of something. Mr. Ratten keeps a stack of brochures like this by the counter at the store. If Ricky and the others do end up going back there, it won't take long for them to put two and two together and realize where we've gone. They might already be on their way."

Cal took a deep breath. "Okay. Clearly, we need to get out of here as soon as possible. The first thing we should do is…" He paused midsentence as a tinkling trill cut through the air.

THIRTEEN

It took Cal a moment to register the source of the ringing. A phone. Since the storm was still raging, it hadn't occurred to him to check if the lines might be back up. A rookie mistake. He swung his leg off the couch and stood. A jolt of pain shot up his body as he staggered forward, caught himself against a chair and then limped across the floor.

"Cal, wait!" Abby called out. "Let me get it."

But he didn't pause. He didn't know if he could stop even if he wanted to. The momentum of his weight lurching forward was propelling his body across the room. If he could maintain his balance for a few more paces, he might be able to reach the large, marble counter for support. Just two more steps. The ache in his calf was mounting, and so was the pulsing pain ricocheting up and down his leg. One more step.

Thud! He slammed into the desk. He reached down and plucked the receiver from its stand.

"Hullo," he panted.

Too late. The person on the other end of the line had hung up. But a steady dial tone vibrated against his ears.

"Cal, are you okay?" Abby set the lanyard down on the table and moved to the spot where he was standing.

He shook his head as he tried to catch his breath. "I'm great. But don't you see? It doesn't matter! The landlines are back up! We can call for backup."

His fingers tapped three digits against the keypad.

"Nine-one-one dispatch. How can I help?"

"Linette. It's me. Cal. Again."

"Cal! Where are you? Is Abby okay? What about Isobel's baby?" There was an anxious edge to Linette's voice.

"We're fine. As we speak, I've got both Abby and the baby in my sight. We're at the Red Fox Lodge."

"The Red Fox Lodge!" Linette repeated in a high voice.

Cal pinched the bridge of his nose with his thumb and his finger and sighed.

"That's right. And we need as much help as you can muster. And also—"

Linette cut him off. "We've had squad cars patrolling the roads ever since Isobel reported the attempted kidnapping, but at the moment, emergency crews can't get past mile marker 103. There's a four-car pileup that's blocking the road. The crews haven't even made it to the bank."

Cal frowned. Given the ferocity of the storm, he wasn't surprised to hear about the accident. Still, it was disappointing to run into yet another roadblock, and a literal one at that. "Okay, Linette, here's what you need to do. Notify the authorities in Fargo. Ask if they can possibly come to our assistance. Let our deputies focus on clearing the road. Anyone coming in from the north will be on Highway 40, so they'll bypass the accident. The state patrol can assist at the bank. Remind them that there will be some explosives so they'll want to bring along a demolition expert. Once we have police on this side of the highway, the next step will be strategizing on how to apprehend the perps. But if I can find a way out of here, my first priority is getting the civilians to safety." He paused. "You got all that?"

"Yes. Okay. I understand." Linette's voice sounded breathless.

"Oh, and Linette, one more thing. Thank you."

He hung up the receiver, scrubbed his hand against his face and turned to face Abby. "Help is on their way."

"I heard." Abby gave him a curious look. "Here. Take my arm. We can talk some more when we get you back to the couch."

"What's the matter?" he asked once he had settled against the cushions. He was having trouble interpreting the quizzical quirk of Abby's mouth. She didn't seem happy. In fact, she seemed downright upset.

He was confused. It wasn't quite time to celebrate, but this was the closest they had been to being rescued all evening. He had faith that Chief Bertram in Fargo would be able to muster a half dozen officers to assist at the scene. It was only about a forty-minute drive under normal conditions. Factoring in the snow-packed roads, the cavalry would arrive in less than an hour.

But Abby still seemed upset.

"What's wrong?" he asked again. "Are you thinking

about Ricky? I was just going to suggest that we head over to the hut with the ATVs. What do you think?"

Abby didn't answer his question. She bent down and began to examine his leg. "You want to know what I think? I think *I* should do that, and that *you* should wait here and rest."

"But what if the keys to start the vehicles aren't on the board or in the ignitions? It'll be a wasted trip if you can't start one up."

"Cal. That little trip of ours to the kitchen caused your stitches to rupture in several places. If you do too much more physical activity, the whole suture could come apart, and your leg will be severely compromised. And you could die if I can't stop the bleeding."

"Huh?" He could see that Abby was apprehensive, but seriously? Why focus on the worst-case scenario?

"Just look at your stiches." She pointed her finger at his leg. There was definitely an edge to her voice.

"What about them?" he asked.

Silence stretched between them for the span of ten seconds.

"I don't think you've been listening to anything I said. Your leg is going to be stressed by a quarter-mile trek through the snow. And that's going to cause a serious problem."

"I'll take it easy. I promise."

"You don't seem to know how to take it easy. I heard you on the phone to Linette. You didn't even mention that you had been shot. You should have told her that you needed an ambulance."

Cal rubbed his jaw. He wasn't quite certain how to

respond. Abby's concern was touching, but at the same time, her offended attitude was perplexing.

"It's standard practice to report when an officer is down," Abby pointed out.

"I guess you're right. But I'm not exactly an officer down. I've already received medical treatment." He offered her his most winning smile, but it didn't work its usual magic. Abby fixed him with a steely glare. He shrugged. "I'm pretty sure that they'll send an ambulance anyway. For the baby."

"Right." She fixed her gaze on the baby asleep on the floor.

He lay his head back against the couch and tried to make sense of Abby's change in attitude. They had been getting along so well. Just ten minutes earlier, it had felt like the two of them were on the same team, and now she was acting like he had committed some great offense by not reporting the fact that he had been shot in the leg.

"C'mon, Abby. What's the real problem here?"

She twisted her hair off the back of her neck and pulled it to one side. "I'm just surprised that you didn't follow procedure. You can't keep pretending that you're operating at one hundred percent and that nothing is wrong."

"I got shot, okay? And the best paramedic in the county stitched me up. Should I have mentioned it on the phone? Maybe. But Linette was upset. And I wanted to get off the line so she could put in the call to Fargo as quickly as possible. Forgive me for not cataloging all of my various injuries."

He instantly regretted his outburst as Abby's back seemed to stiffen.

"I guess we'll have to agree to disagree about what you can and can't do because of your injuries. Maybe I'm just stressed and need to close my eyes for a minute to think."

Remorse flooded his senses. Of course, she was tired. On top of everything else, she'd been taking care of both him and the baby. Why hadn't he realized that she needed a break?

He lugged himself back into a sitting position.

"I'm sorry. Yes. You lie down and rest. I'm going to move over to that big lounge chair by the window. That way, I can keep an eye on the baby and watch the road as well. And when you're done resting, we can talk about finding a way to track down an ATV."

"Okay." She stretched out on the couch, folded her arms over her chest and closed her eyes.

Cal watched her for a moment. Then he pulled himself upright and, by hanging on to the surrounding furniture, slowly made his way across the room. He settled himself on the large recliner and picked up the pair of binoculars from a basket by the chair. He swiveled sideways and adjusted the focus toward the highway. Watching the road for suspicious vehicles would keep his mind from straying toward other thoughts. Like thoughts about the woman trying to sleep just a few feet away from him.

It wasn't that she was beautiful. Which she was. But it was so much more than that. He'd always admired her strength, but tonight he had seen her kindness, her selflessness, her faith. In fact, maybe he needed to add one more item to the bucket list he kept tucked in the back of his mind. It was the resolve to finally open his heart again. Something had happened between him and Abby tonight, something that had forced him to recognize that what they had shared in the past few hours was more than friendship. And he was ready to risk finding out if Abby felt the same way.

He was about to set the binoculars back on their stand when a movement in the distance caught his eye. He peered through the lenses. Was that a cloud of snow from an approaching vehicle? His gut clenched, and the hairs on the back of his neck stood on edge. There was no way that the Fargo officers could be here already. And besides, it wasn't a police vehicle that was approaching. Not an official one anyway. It was still far away, but he'd recognize the shape and the color anywhere. It was his own blue F-150. The truck he had left parked in the bank lot.

And the kidnappers had his keys.

Abby kept her eyes screwed shut. There was no way that she was going to fall asleep, but Cal didn't need to know that. Pretending to take a nap had just seemed like an effective way to take a couple of minutes to think things through.

Why had she acted so childish and petulant, chiding Cal for not requesting that an ambulance be sent to the lodge? Usually, she kept her emotions in tighter control. So why had she allowed herself to get so upset? She clenched her fingers into a tight fist. She knew why.

It was because she was scared and angry. Scared that Cal's injuries were potentially life-threatening. Angry that he didn't seem to care.

Maybe it was none of her business. But when Cal had told her about Shannon, it had felt for a moment like it was a bridge to something more. An understanding. A bond. A deeper connection. But if Cal continued to ignore her medical advice, there was a very good chance that there might not be a happy ending for any of them, least of all for Cal.

And the thought of something happening to him upset her to her very core.

"Abby, wake up!" Cal was suddenly beside her, whispering in her ear. "We need to get out here and find a place to hide. Ricky and the others are headed down the road."

"What?" Even though she hadn't been asleep, a grogginess had dulled her senses, and a lethargy invaded her limbs. But all of a sudden, Cal's words penetrated her weary brain. Her eyes sprang open. "They found us?"

"Yeah. They're halfway down the entry road."

Abby leaped up, her heart sinking in her chest. How had the kidnappers discovered them so quickly? It didn't matter. They needed to move fast and find someplace safe to hide.

"I know," she said. "We should go into the kitchen! It's big and dark with lots of nooks and crannies. We can probably find a place to hole up in there." She slipped the sleeping baby back into the sling and hurried to scoop up their supplies with her other hand. Maybe if the lobby looked deserted, the kidnappers would give up and start their search in the cabins along the shore. A loud crash echoed from the other side of the room. She turned her head and saw that, on his way across the lobby, Cal had knocked down a lamp. Her heart squeezed in her chest. She raced over to the spot where he was standing and bent to pick up the fallen light.

"I've got it!" she said. "Just keep going."

But when she tried to lift the lamp, the diapers and box of formula dropped from her grip.

"Let it go, Abby. There isn't time to worry about that."

She started to turn around, but then she stopped. Wouldn't a tipped over light confirm that something was amiss? She swiveled and retraced her steps. Setting down the baby, she lifted the lamp back onto the table. Then she bundled the infant and his supplies back into her arms and followed Cal out of the lobby.

Dread thudded in her chest. She had been wrong. The dining room, with its stripped-down tables and stacked chairs, didn't offer many places to hide. And in the kitchen, the shelves at the bottom of the counters were far too open to conceal two adults and a baby.

Abby scampered past the small refrigerator where they had found the English muffins and headed into the pantry. But the narrow shelves were far too flimsy to hold their weight.

"Waaaa! Waaaa!"

No! Not now! She glanced down. The baby had his lip pushed out and his face was crumpled and red.

"Shh," she whispered.

The little boy gave another wail of distress. How could a child this small have this much lung capacity?

"Abby, in here!"

Cal motioned toward the front of a large walk-in freezer.

"This seems to be our only option. Don't worry. There's a latch on the inside that we can open when we're ready to come out."

With a lurch, the metal door creaked open on its hinges. Abby looked back down at the baby. She didn't like the idea of exposing an infant to such cold temperatures again. But on the plus side, it was a soundproof solution to their problem. Of course, it would be impossible to know for sure when the coast was clear, but the thick walls would muffle the sounds of a crying infant. She hesitated for a moment and then followed Cal inside. As the door swung closed, they both let out a sigh.

But her relief was short-lived. The arctic temperature was already causing her to shiver. The baby didn't seem to appreciate his new cold environment, either, as his cries turned into howls. She patted his back in a desperate attempt to comfort him, but it only increased his distress.

"He's really cold," she said, pressing him closer to her body for warmth. "And he's resisting all my attempts to settle him down."

"Let me give it try." Cal's voice sounded deeper in the enclosed space.

She lifted the baby out of the sling and reached out in the darkness to find Cal's hand. He took the infant from her arms and began moving back and forth, singing something soft under his breath. Abby took a couple steps away from them and listened.

"The Wheels on the Bus" was an odd choice to sing to a baby in a freezer, but the tune worked its magic. After a few minutes, the baby stopped wailing and settled down.

"Abby," Cal whispered. "Come back over here and stand next to me. I've got a plan. But we both need to be in position over here by the door."

She hurried to close the gap between them.

"Good. Now I'm going to lay the little guy down on the shelf." He clicked on the flashlight he had grabbed in the store and then quickly flicked it off. "He should stay warm enough, swaddled up tight in his blanket. You can put the rest of the baby stuff on this shelf. Stand as close as you can to me, and I'll explain the plan."

Abby moved closer. She felt the warmth from Cal's side as she pressed beside him.

"The door opens in," he said.

Huh? She waited for him to elaborate.

"If they check inside the freezer, we'll be blocked by the door. So as long as our little buddy here doesn't decide to have another crying fit, we may be able to escape detection."

Abby considered this. Cal's plan was based on the assumption that the kidnappers wouldn't take the time to enter the freezer. And that the baby would remain asleep. It seemed risky, especially since they didn't even know for certain that Ricky and his crew had entered the building. For all they knew, they had bypassed the main lodge and gone on to search the smaller cabins.

She could feel her body tightening as doubts crowded her mind.

Cal reached down and cupped her hand in his own. "Trust me."

Abby closed her eyes. Trust. Faith. That was what she needed now. *Help us, God.* Her heart squeezed in her chest.

Seconds ticked by as they waited. Within the insulated wall, she couldn't hear anything, but the not-knowing was almost worse than being found. Cal squeezed her hand as she prayed for courage and protection.

Just as she was about to suggest they give up waiting and escape the cold—*clunk*—the door flew open and crashed against her forehead. She bit back a yelp of pain, forcing herself to stay silent as a triangle of light opened on the space.

"Nobody's in here. Maybe we should check upstairs."

Abby's heart quaked. She didn't recognize the husky voice of the interloper, but it might have been Tomas, the man Cal shot in the gunfight at the bank. For a while, it seemed that he was down for the count. But that no longer seemed to be the case.

"I'll meet you on the steps," the man with the deep voice spoke again. The freezer was once again plunged into darkness as the door thumped closed.

For several minutes, she and Cal remained like statues, fixed in place. After a couple of minutes passed without a sound, she felt Cal's body shift as he lifted the baby back into his arms.

She slowly exhaled as her pounding pulse returned to normal. "It worked!" she breathed.

"It did," Cal whispered back.

Abby realized with a start that her fingers were still entwined with Cal's. Her breath hitched in her throat as she pulled her hand back and took a step to the side.

"Cal? I think the man who checked the freezer was Tomas. Which means there are four of them now, and they probably all have guns." She drew in a deep breath. "So, what do we do next?"

"Finding a new hiding place is our first priority. Right now, they're just doing a cursory search. But when they don't find us, they'll become more methodical. If they check the kitchen again, I don't think we'll escape their notice twice. Besides, it's too cold to stay in here much longer."

"So?" She let the question hang.

"So," Cal replied, "I'll take a peek out of the door to make sure no one's around. Then we'll need to make a run for it."

Abby stared at him. *Make a run for it?* How did he think that was going to work with a baby and a sheriff with a shot leg?

She swallowed her question.

Because Cal was already reaching for the handle on the freezer door.

FOURTEEN

The latch clicked open. Cal handed Abby the baby as he inched forward to peer through the slit. The kitchen was as dark and quiet as a tomb. Tomas was gone, at least for the moment.

This was their chance. When Ricky and the others finished on the upper level, they would undoubtedly return to do another, more thorough sweep of the dining room and kitchen.

Cal snuck a look behind him at Abby, who held the baby in her arms. In the dimness of the space, it was hard to read her expression, but her dark eyes shone like black pools, reflecting a wariness that he had seen earlier on her face.

He whispered, "We need to find a way out of here without being seen."

"Right. There ought to be a back door around here somewhere. Places like this usually have a separate entrance for deliveries and staff."

Bingo! If they could find another exit, they could head to one of the cabins. A twinge of uncertainly pinged across his brain, but he brushed it away. Staying one step ahead of the kidnappers was hardly a long-term solution, but at this point, it was just a matter of running out the clock. The place was huge, so that was an advantage. And the police were on their way.

Cal took a step forward, and a jolt of pain rocketed up his leg. This wasn't going to be as easy as he thought, but staying put was not an option. "C'mon," he said. He held the freezer door open and waited for Abby to step through.

"Wait." Abby tilted her head to the left, toward the far wall. "When I moved the snowmobile, I saw a dumpster along this side of the building. The delivery door is usually close to the garbage. Let's go this way."

Cal turned and followed Abby. Trust her to have noticed the dumpster. If she hadn't become a paramedic, she would have made a great cop. Observant. Brave. Intrepid. Qualities he looked for in all new recruits. He shook his head. Was he seriously cataloguing Abby's virtues again? It wasn't as if he needed more reasons to like her. He had gone too far down that road already. He wiggled the fingers she had been clutching just a few minutes earlier. That had been nice, even though she had pulled away once the danger passed.

A bump in the carpet caused him to stumble and another agonizing bolt of pain pierced his leg. Time seemed to stop as he felt himself tumbling forward in slow motion even as a host of recriminations flashed through his brain. He should have been watching his steps rather than thinking about Abby. He should have focused more on noticing what was in front of him instead of remembering what it felt like to hold Abby's hand.

A second later, his body slammed into something softer than the floor. And then he was being pushed back up as Abby slowly unfurled from the crouched position beneath him.

He grasped the edge of the counter and pulled himself the rest of the way up. A moment later, Abby stood facing him. She was breathing hard. His own heart pounded like a jackhammer in his chest. The ache in his leg was worse than ever. But, even as his brain registered the pain, his mind couldn't focus on anything except the woman standing in front of him. Their eyes locked, and he caught and held her stare for the beat of half a second.

"That was close," she whispered.

"Too close," he breathed back.

His ears strained to hear the sound of footsteps rushing down the stairs, but all was silent. Eerily so. Before he could think twice, he pulled Abby toward him and pressed his lips against hers. It was a gesture born of pure instinct, but it felt surprisingly right. Even more shocking was the fact that Abby returned his kiss before pulling back from his embrace.

"No man left behind," she mumbled. "C'mon. We've got to move."

She turned her gaze away from him and resumed her trek through the darkened kitchen. Cal kept his eyes trained forward. Maybe later he could explain why kissing her in that moment had felt so right. But for now, he needed to concentrate. There was no way he was going to make another misstep, even though the ache in his leg had intensified tenfold. Already, a damp warmth was spreading down his leg. But that didn't matter. He needed to get Abby and the baby as far away from the kidnappers as fast as he possibly could.

Anxiety pitted in his gut as they made their way past the shelves in the pantry and an open storage bin along the back wall. There were still sounds coming from the rooms upstairs, and with each moment that passed, they were that much closer to being discovered before they made their escape.

"Found it!" Abby whispered.

Thank you, God!

Grasping the handle, he pushed open the door. A thin strand of gray had appeared along the edge of the eastern sky. In less than an hour, the dim shadows of early morning would lighten into day. And there was the dumpster, just as Abby had said. And the snowmobile was only about thirty yards away. Should they climb aboard in the hope of making a quick escape? No, it was too risky. It was almost out of gas, and the sound of the engine would cause Ricky and the others to rush down the stairs. But what was the alternative? Heading for the hut with the ATVs was out of the question. It had been difficult enough to cover the short distance from the lobby to the kitchen.

He shifted his gaze across the landscape, and dread washed over him. The nearest cabin was at least eighty yards away. The pathway would take them through open terrain. And they would undoubtedly leave footprints in the snow.

Could he make it without being seen? Probably not

at his current pace. But Abby and the baby could. Especially if he provided a distraction.

"You go ahead," he whispered. "I'm headed back inside to buy you some time."

Abby fixed him with a stubborn glare. "Excuse me? Just what exactly are you suggesting?"

"It's the only way, Abby. You have to see that. You have a real shot of making it to safety. But I'm a liability. There's no chance that I can reach the cabin without being seen. But I can still protect you if you'll do as I say."

Abby quirked her lips. "I don't think so, Cal. We've gotten this far working together, and we still have one or two more moves to put into play. At this point, Ricky and his thugs can't find us, and for all they know, we could be anywhere at the lodge." She shifted the baby to one arm and looped the other around Cal's waist. "Plus, the police will be here before we know it. So, why would we give up now? What are we waiting for? Let's go."

There wasn't time to argue. He threaded his hand around Abby for support. Summoning up a reserve of strength he didn't know he had, he increased his speed to a slow jog as she matched his pace toward the cabin's front door.

"We made it," he panted as he stepped up onto the porch. "But I left the key ring on the desk. I guess that means we'll have to do this the hard way." He pushed open the screen. Then he leaned forward and slammed his body into the lightweight inner door. The wood creaked, but the hinges gave way as the door crashed inward and he landed, sprawled in the middle of the living room floor.

Ouch. That hurt.

"Well, that was fun." He turned his head and offered Abby a cheeky grin.

But his joy was short-lived as he glanced back out through the screen door.

Like signposts guiding a hiker along a trail, bright red splotches of blood staining the snow under their footprints had marked their route from the kitchen to the porch.

Abby's heart twinged in her chest. There was something incredibly appealing about Cal's crooked smile as he looked up at her from his position on the floor. Except that he was no longer smiling. His jaw was clenched and his lips were curled into an anxious grimace.

She set the baby down on the braided carpet for a quick check. Good news. After everything they had been through, the little guy seemed as healthy as ever. She laid a hand against his forehead. Even his temperature felt right.

Satisfied that the baby was warm and comfortable, she turned to her other patient who had pushed himself upright and was slowly making his way toward the door. His hair had twigs in it. His arms were covered in small scratches. His clothes were wet and his pants had a deep red stain where he had been shot. She put up her hand to stop him. "Where are you going? Your stitches are bleeding and torn."

"I can't worry about that. Look."

He pointed out toward the open door and the footprints and droplets of blood that marked their path in the snow.

Abby pulled in a deep breath. This was not good. But it also wasn't catastrophic. It was likely that the kidnappers were still inside the lodge. They hadn't expanded their search outside the main building—at least not yet. And the screen entry to the cabin was still intact. From a distance, it would be hard to tell that the inner door was off its hinges, especially if they leaned it back upright. But it was only a matter of time before one of their pursuers noticed their tracks and followed them to the cabin. She needed to find some way to cover their bloody trail with snow.

"Cal, you can't go back out there," she said. Her tone was sharp, but it had the intended effect. Cal turned to face her, his eyes weary and deep creases furrowing his brow.

"I have to," he said.

"No, Cal. Think about it. Your leg is still bleeding. You'll make it worse."

He took a deep breath, and his entire body seemed to shudder. "But we need to do something."

"I agree. And the first thing we have to do is have you sit down so I can give your leg a quick check." She guided him toward the sofa in the center of the cabin. He sat down with a thump, and she bent to examine the wound.

Cal's leg didn't look as bad as she had expected. A thin bubble of relief expanded in her chest. "It looks like you gouged out part of the suture and split about five of the stitches. But the rest ought to hold, at least for the time being."

"Great. So, I can go take care of those footprints." Cal started to stand up.

"No. You stay here and watch the baby, and I'll go outside." She took two steps toward the cabin's front door.

"No." Cal's voice was a low growl, and there was something in his eyes that stopped her in her tracks.

"It's the only way." She grabbed the three bath towels that were laid out on the counter. "I know that you think I am a civilian and that it is your duty to protect me. But we need to play to our strengths." She tossed one of the towels to Cal. "Press this against your leg to try to stop the bleeding." She tucked the other two towels into the pocket of her sweatshirt and headed toward the door.

"Abby, wait."

She paused and turned to face him.

"You talk about duty," he said, "but that's only part of it. Keeping everyone safe is my job, but that's not all. After everything that's happened tonight—" he spread his hands out in a hopeless gesture "—it's been so much more."

"We'll talk about that later, Cal. But, for now, you need to relax. I've got this." She turned back toward the door.

"Wait," Cal called after her a second time, and once more, she turned to face him.

"What?" she said. "Really, Cal. You don't need to worry about me. You're the one who…"

Her words trailed off as Cal pushed himself upright and limped toward her. As he reached for her hand, there was an intensity in his eyes that caused her heart to pound even harder in her chest.

"I get it, Abby. I don't want to argue anymore. Just be careful. I don't know what I'd do if something happened to you."

She released a long breath and nodded her head. She wanted to hold on to this moment, to freeze time just for a second, but she knew that was impossible. She untwined her fingers from Cal's hand and headed toward the threshold, willing her eyes not to turn for one last look at the man who had been her constant companion throughout the long night and into the new day. She couldn't—she wouldn't—let herself think about the promise that had been in Cal's eyes, at least not until the kidnappers were in custody and the baby was safe. For now, she had a job to do, and she needed to train her eyes on the path ahead.

No doubt she stood out against the white backdrop with her dark hair and black hoodie. But if she moved quickly and stayed low, she might be able to avoid detection. With the two towels wrapped around her hands, she patted on a fresh layer of flakes over the first couple of drops along the path, taking time to dust some over their footprints in the snow. The crimson stains disappeared beneath the whiteness as did the shallow depressions of their tracks. She took a step forward and did the same thing again. It was slow going, but gradually she covered the distance to the lodge's kitchen door.

She glanced back toward the cabin. Had she done a good enough job obscuring their trail? Maybe. But she needed to do something more to protect Cal and the baby. But what?

Ever since her dad's accident, she had known that she was called to help others. It was her gift. Her role in God's plan. For a long time, she believed that He had planted her here to adopt Davey and give him a home. But now there was another child who needed her help even more desperately. She thought of Isobel's little boy, sound asleep in the cabin. A sense of peace settled in her heart, replacing the adrenaline rush from seconds earlier. The anxiety she had felt all evening evaporated. She knew what she had to do next.

She looked up at the early-morning sky. Dawn was breaking in a firmament sprinkled with hundreds of tiny lights. When she was little, she'd imagined that the stars were souls looking down on her and watching her from heaven. The biggest and brightest one was always her father. The memory brought her comfort. And for a moment, all seemed calm and right. This was where she was supposed to be. Her entire life had been building toward this moment.

Her eyes darted to the left and the right as she improvised her next move.

She would hop on the snowmobile and lure Ricky and the others to follow her, either on foot or in the SUV. If all went well, she could lead her pursuers to the middle of the lake. But even if the motor stalled out and she didn't make it that far, she could at least buy Cal time to find a good hiding place for himself and the baby.

Cal had told her not to take any risks, but this was a calculated one that could save them all. She kept her body low and flat against the exterior wall as she crept around the back of the lodge toward the abandoned snowmobile. She bundled up the towels and shoved them under her sweatshirt and yanked hard on the pull start. Nothing. She lengthened her stance and tried again. This time, the engine sprang to life with an angry growl. She straddled the seat and revved the motor. If this was going to work, she needed to make sure she was heard.

A second later, the back door banged open and Max appeared, pistol in hand.

She didn't waste another moment. She pressed down on the accelerator, flattened her body against the seat, and shot off toward the lake with Max running behind her in pursuit. Her goal was to lure him as far away from the cabin as possible, but the snowmobile wasn't cooperating. It slowed to a crawl as the engine popped and sputtered. No surprise there. The needle on the gas gauge pointed to empty. She was running on fumes, and Max was getting closer by the minute. She turned her head and saw that a second man had joined in the chase. Even from thirty yards away, she could tell it was Ricky.

The distance between them dwindled even more as the snowmobile jerked to a shuttering stop.

She leaped off the vehicle and sprinted toward the dock. She was still ahead of her pursuers. But as she cast a quick glance in the direction of the cabin where

Cal was hiding with the baby, her heart dropped. She may have distracted Max and Ricky, but that wasn't good enough. Martina was approaching the cabin's front door.

Abby picked up her speed and headed for the boat-house. As she rounded the corner of the open pavilion in the front, her path was blocked by a maze of storage racks stocked full of canoes and kayaks. Her breath hitched out in short, desperate puffs as fatigue slowed her limbs. Behind her came the thud of boots against the snow. She didn't know how much farther she could run, but if she didn't take evasive action, her pursuers would catch up to her soon.

She stepped up onto the first rung of the metal stand and began to climb up the side of the rack. The metal poles teetered under her weight, but she continued moving toward the top. Shifting her body forward, she propped her head on the underside of one seat and her legs on the other so that she was lying in the shelter of an overturned red canoe.

She closed her eyes and began to pray.

FIFTEEN

Cal held his breath as the clamor of slamming doors drifted up the stairs. Martina seemed to know that he was hiding somewhere inside the cabin, and she was determined to search every nook and cranny until he was found.

He had been watching out the living room window when Abby took off on the snowmobile. For a moment, he had felt hopeful as she cut a straight route toward the dock. Maybe there was more gas in the tank than he thought. But his heart had dropped when the door to the main lodge had flown open, and Ricky and Max had taken off in pursuit, leaving Martina behind to search the cabins.

Beginning with the one where he was holed up with the baby.

There had been no time to consider all of the options or to make a logical plan. Operating on gut instinct, he had grabbed the little boy and hobbled up the stairs, making his way toward the bathroom at the far side of the loft. He climbed into the bathtub and pulled the curtain closed behind them just as the floorboards shook with the thud of footsteps. Judging from the sounds, Martina was inside the cabin and in the process of opening and closing every closet and cabinet door.

How long before she finished on the first floor and headed up to the upper level? The place was small. It wouldn't take her more than a couple of minutes to search the downstairs. But between the baby in his arms and his hurt leg, he had limited options when it came to engineering an escape. A bitter sense of failure pitted in his stomach. There were so many things he should have done differently. Sure, in the past few years, he had suffered his share of self-doubts. But even as his marriage crumbled, he had remained assured of his competence on the job. He was a good cop, and he knew it. That confidence had led him to apply for the sheriff position in Dagger Lake and allowed him to make a fresh start. His faith had grown, forcing him to remember that he was a precious child of God.

But he suddenly felt unmoored in a vast ocean of doubt amid a raging storm. He was the sheriff, and yet he hadn't been able to protect Abby or the baby. And where was God in all this? All evening he had been praying, but it didn't seem like God was listening. He shouldn't be thinking like this. A better Christian wouldn't let his faith falter. So yet again, he had struggled and failed.

No! He tightened his jaw and balled his hands into fists. He wasn't going to despair. God was with him. With a prayer for guidance, he set the baby down and climbed out of the tub. Then he braced his hands against the shower rod and pulled with all his might. With a loud crack, the pole snapped off the wall. He dumped the curtain on the floor and waited.

Anger washed through him. He was the sheriff. And he wasn't going down without a fight.

After a few minutes, he heard the tread of approaching footsteps. He gripped the metal bar in his hands and kept his eyes glued to the door. Seconds ticked by before the knob began to turn. He didn't wait for Martina to step inside. He yanked the door open and walloped the shower rod down on her head. With a stunned look of surprise, she hit the ground, unconscious but still breathing.

He rolled the shower curtain into a makeshift rope and bound her hands to the pipe beneath the sink. Bending down, he scooped up her pistol and tucked it into the back pocket of his pants.

Now it was time to track down Abby.

But first he had to find a safe place to stow the baby. He picked up the precious bundle and maneuvered back down the stairs. It looked like a cyclone had been through the living room and kitchen. Chairs were tipped over, and lamps leaned sideways on the floor. But the disarray might work to his advantage. If one of the other criminals came into the cabin, they might assume that these rooms had already been examined and give them a pass. His eyes skimmed around the room, but nothing jumped out as a safe place to hide the baby.

He shuffled into the bedroom. Martina had made a mess here, too. The bedding was thrown on the ground, and the bed was shoved flat against the wall. Or was it? He limped forward for a closer examination. The footing was wider than the actual frame, leaving a small gap between the bed and wall. Kissing the baby on the top of his head, Cal gently laid him in the crack. And then he backed out of the room.

Was he doing the right thing? Doubts assailed his mind. Leaving the infant alone in the cabin was a potentially reckless move. He weighed the pros and cons of strapping the little guy on his back, but all things considered, the hiding place by the bed seemed more secure.

With a final prayer for guidance, he limped out the door.

He still had to deal with a badly wounded leg, but now he had Martina's pistol clutched tightly in his hand.

Abby lay motionless under the red canoe, listening to Max and Ricky tipping over boats as they worked their way through the racks. With each thunderous boom that assailed her ears, her hiding place felt even more claustrophobic. And it was clear that Ricky and Max were getting closer. Her hands trembled, and her fingers clenched as she recalled the sensation of holding Cal's hand in the freezer. She had been afraid then, too, but Cal's presence had comforted her. She wished he were here now. Realization dawned. She wanted a partner. She needed a partner. It wasn't weak to want to have someone to share your burdens, to help you in times of sorrow and to be there with you in moments of joy.

Thud! The last thump felt like it was right underneath her. She unhooked her legs from the underside of the back bench and pulled her head out, as well. Fastening her fingers around the side of the canoe, she set her feet along the overturned bottom and waited to see what the men would going to do. She wasn't ready to give up. God had showed her something precious tonight, and she was going to do everything she could to save it. For too long, she had rejected the idea of love and companionship, choosing to prize her independence and self-sufficiency. But now she wanted more. Maybe life wasn't about choices. Maybe it was about possibilities. Possibilities of embarking on a life with someone beside her, not trying to achieve everything alone. Not that she had ever been truly alone.

Please, God, help me. Stay with me as you always have. Protect me and keep me safe.

"She's in here for sure." Max's deep voice was instantly recognizable.

"Maybe so, but she's trapped. And when we find her, she'll have nowhere to go." Ricky's scornful laugh reverberated through the space. "Leave her to me, Max. I can handle one woman on my own. Go back to the lodge. Tomas might have found the others hiding somewhere on the main floor. If not, both of you should check to see if Martina needs help searching the cabins."

Abby pulled in a long breath as Max's footsteps faded away. She flexed her leg and prepared to make her move. Her timing had to be perfect if she was going to stay one step ahead in the chase. There was a loud thump as the canoe below her slid off the rack. Now! Now was her chance.

Leveraging the power of her limbs, she pushed the

canoe onto Ricky and then rolled in the opposite direction. She landed in the snow, pulled herself up and took off running.

Shouts echoed behind her as she reversed course. In her arms, she clutched the two loose bath towels. Maybe from far away it would look like she was holding a baby.

Her pulse pounded as she tried to run faster, but she couldn't make her feet move quickly enough to gain any ground on Ricky. For every two steps forward, she slid back one as the soles of her shoes lost their grip on the slippery snow.

"Stop," a cold voice ordered.

Ricky was close. Too close.

But she ignored the command, lunging to the right in hopes of gaining an advantage with a haphazard route.

A shot rang out. A bullet whizzed by, inches from her head.

"I told you to stop. I will not repeat myself again. If you want to save the life of our son, you will obey me."

Our son. Ricky assumed that she was Isobel. It made sense. She and Isobel were approximately the same height. And throughout the evening, she had been wearing a hoodie that obscured her features and covered her hair.

Clasping the bath towels even tighter to her chest, she stopped, but she kept her face turned from his sight.

"That's better. I would have thought you would have learned by now that nothing good comes from defying me. But then you must not have known me very well if you imagined that you could leave me. My darling

wife, did you really think that I would let you go? Or
that I would allow you to take my child away from me?"

Abby remained still, her head bent and her body
poised. Her chest heaved as she fought to catch her
breath. What to do? What to do? The situation had gone
from bad to worse in a hurry. Her attempt to lure the
kidnappers away from the cabin had failed, and Cal and
the baby were now in danger of being discovered by
Martina. All because she had to go off and do things
her own way.

Blood pounded through her veins, and panic clouded
her judgment. If Ricky got any closer, she would take
off running. But for now, she would stay where she was.
Praying that Cal would find her. Praying that the police
would arrive in time to save them.

"Just who do you think you are? When I met you,
you were a nobody. A nothing. I took the time to show
you the world, teach you about the finer things in life.
And how do you repay me? You run away. You must
have known that I would hunt you down. I wonder if
you even wanted me to find you. Why else would you
have selected the hometown of your oldest friend? You
should have realized that I had the money and the re-
sources to discover your hiding place, no matter how
far you might go."

There was no way to respond to his grotesque threats
and accusations. All she could do was clamp her lips
tight against the force of his ugly words.

"Imagine my surprise when I discovered you were
pregnant. I had been prepared to take you back. You
are young and foolish. And even fools are allowed one

indiscretion. No more. A man in my situation doesn't allow betrayal. Not without retribution. Regrettably for you, you committed two transgressions, running away and attempting to separate me from my own flesh and blood. I knew of your whereabouts for months, but I couldn't compromise the health of my child by seizing you too soon. So I allowed you to remain here, unaware that I was watching you and monitoring your pregnancy. And when the time was right, I commenced my plan. You do realize that everything that happened tonight occurred because of me, right?"

He paused, and she held her breath.

"I asked you a question. Answer me."

She nodded her head, praying that that would be enough. The acknowledgment seemed to appease him, at least for the moment. But how long could she continue the masquerade?

"Even your manager friend winning a vacation that required her to leave you alone at the bank. All me. Of course, I didn't count on that idiot cowboy shooting the doctor, but it didn't matter in the end. You thought you knew me so well, but you don't know anything at all.

"You are wondering why we staged a bank robbery instead of snatching you from your apartment and taking my son? You were never very good at putting two and two together, were you, my dear? That's why you needed me. But I digress. I realized that if I were to abduct you, your friend Tessa would alert the police. Nothing I couldn't handle, but an unnecessary annoyance, nonetheless. I determined that it would be easier to arrange to induce your labor at the bank. And once you had the baby, blow up the whole building with you inside. We'd use so much C-4 that there would be no evidence left, no bodies to examine, no trace of what went down. The fire department would assume that it was a robbery gone wrong, and no one would be any wiser. That's what we in the business world call win-win."

Win-win? What sort of person talked about the death of innocent human beings in such a heartless way? A wave of pity for Isobel surged in her heart even as she leaned forward and focused on a point straight ahead—a stand of pines set back in the shadows. If she took off sprinting, what were the chances of reaching it without getting shot?

But then what? She could hide, but her tracks in the snow would be easy to follow. Besides, it would be a challenge to outrun a bullet. And Ricky looked like the kind of man who didn't often miss when he took aim. But would he dare fire at her if he thought she was holding his son? It was a risk she might have to take.

Yet still she hesitated and once again considered the odds. Her ears strained to catch the faint hum of vehicles approaching from the distance, but still a long way off. The police? The sound was getting louder, but would help arrive too late?

But there was something else, too.

A muffled shuffling in the snow, boots squeaking against the frozen ground as someone approached from the east.

Ricky didn't seem to notice. His anger would not be denied. He raised his voice to be heard above the howling wind. "I do have bad news for you, my dear Isobel.

This is where you and I say goodbye. I can't forgive what you did to me. Nor will I forget. And I don't like living with a grudge. It's better this way. You hand over my son, and then I kill you. But you can rest assured that once you are dead, I will mourn your passing for all the world to see how deeply I loved my precious wife."

He took a step toward her. Then another. He was so close that she could almost feel the hatred in his breath. Run! Run! Her brain registered the impulse, but her feet remained cemented in place.

A heavy hand clamped down on her shoulder, and thick, powerful fingers dug into her flesh. Ricky spun her around to face him, his eyes dark and fierce, and his lips drawn back to reveal a row of glistening white teeth.

"You aren't Isobel!" he roared at the sight of her face.

Tears trickled down her face. Before she took off on the snowmobile, she had been prepared to die. But now, with freedom so close, she was no longer resigned to her fate. She wanted to live. She wanted to see Cal again. To hug Isobel and to hold her baby. To be a mother to Davey. And even as hopelessness clawed at her senses, her body ached with a longing as deep and powerful as any she had ever known. But she had waited too long, and now there would be no second chances.

Out of the corner of her eye, she could see Ricky's finger twitching on the trigger. At this close a distance, he wouldn't miss.

But before she could close her eyes to whisper another prayer, Cal lunged by her. Both men fell to the ground.

As the two scuffled, Abby dove toward the gleaming metal reflected against the whiteness of the snow.

Ricky was on top, and then Cal, each man fighting to gain the advantage. In the background, a wail of sirens cut through the air. Three squad cars with red lights blazing raced toward the lodge.

Her fingers shook as they closed around the trigger. "Stop," she said, pointing the pistol at Ricky's chest. "Stop, or I'll shoot."

Ricky turned to meet her stare, his dark eyes daring her to make good on her threat.

The smirk slid from his face as an armed deputy reached her side. A second man joined him, and then a third. With four barrels fixed on him, Ricky raised his hands in surrender.

And then it was all over.

The nightmare had come to an end. Just like that.

More police arrived at the scene. Ricky was handcuffed and shoved into the back of one squad car while Martina was shuffled into the back seat of another. An ambulance arrived, and Max and Tomas were loaded onto gurneys, both with gunshot wounds in the leg.

For the moment at least, Cal was refusing to leave the scene and go to the hospital. The EMTs had strongly suggested that he rest in the ambulance while they applied temporary glue to his frayed stitches. But after twenty minutes of recuperation, he had insisted that he was needed to coordinate the situation on site. There was evidence to gather. A crime scene to preserve. And if she knew Sheriff Cal Stanek, it would be a thorough investigation because there was no way that Ricky was going to walk this time.

One of the detectives, a tall, gangly kid with a buzz cut, took her arm and led her across the grounds. As she passed a group of police gathered by the dock, her eyes met Cal's for one fleeting moment, lingering as they both acknowledged that there was still much to be said.

And before she knew it, the baby was back in her arms, and she was being tucked onto a gurney in the back of a second ambulance that had just arrived.

She felt relief. And gratitude. But also the inklings of something else. In that last glimpse of Cal, a new sort of feeling stirred in her heart.

Something much deeper than friendship.

But that was too much to think about just now.

SIXTEEN

Six hours later, lying on an examination table at North Memorial Medical Center, Cal rolled his neck against the back of his shoulders and readjusted his position. The doctor was sure taking her time signing off on his discharge. Not that he didn't appreciate her thoroughness. But he had already spent more than two hours being poked and prodded and questioned and fawned over. Two hours undergoing X-rays and tests, suffering through the removal of his stitches, the sterilization of his bullet wound and the piercing sensation of clean sutures. At least this time, his skin had been numbed. But those two long hours had delayed his visit to the three people he most wanted to see.

He flexed his leg as it dangled over the side of the table and released a pent-up sigh. "So, am I good to go, Doc?"

Dr. Callie Lundgren looked up from her clipboard and frowned. "To tell you the truth, Sheriff, I'm not comfortable releasing you. A gunshot is a traumatic shock to the body. It's a wonder that those stitches held up as well as they did. The paramedic who did the work probably saved your life."

He nodded. He knew all that. In fact, the paramedic was a big part of the reason he was so eager to get going.

But the doctor hadn't finished her lecture. "And I haven't even mentioned the lump on the back of your head. I prefer to keep a patient with this type of injury twenty-four hours for observation to make sure that we aren't dealing with a concussion."

He swiveled sideways and lowered his body down from the table. No way was he extending his hospital stay any longer than necessary. "Thanks, Doc, but I need to get out of here. I have a jail full of criminals who need to be processed. Not to mention a mountain of paperwork waiting on my desk." He pointed to a set of crutches leaning against the wall and offered her his most charming smile. "If I promise to take it easy and stay off my leg, will you let me go?"

For a moment, it seemed that she might refuse his request. She frowned and tapped her fingernails against the clipboard, studying his impatient stance.

"While I can't recommend you returning to work, I'm not about to tell the hero of Dagger Lake that he can't leave the hospital. But remember that you need to go home and rest. Is there someone you can ask to stay with you and check on you every couple of hours to make sure you're okay? You need to step back and let someone else take the lead on the investigation. Your deputies can handle things, at least for the next few days."

He raised his right hand in a mock salute as he backed out the door. "Will do. Thanks, Doc."

"And I want to see you back here in two weeks," she called out after him.

Crutches tucked under his arms, he shuffled down the corridor. The hall was wide and, for the time being, empty, and he was glad to have the opportunity to be alone. He needed time to think. The doctor was right. His body was craving rest. But despite everything, he didn't feel sleepy. He felt restless. He felt excited. He felt alive.

Being chased by hardened criminals across the countryside caused a man to reevaluate his priorities.

Like this weekend. If he hadn't stopped at the bank intending to cash his check, he would be holed up right now in a seven-by-nine-foot shack, line dangling into the water. And he still could be, if he wanted to. Although he had already phoned to explain his absence for the weekend, he knew that his Dad would be happy if he made a surprise appearance.

But ice fishing was no longer at the top of his to-do list.

Everything had changed the moment he realized he might lose the woman he loved.

No, he knew exactly where he was headed. First, the hospital gift shop.

He crutched along the first-floor hallway and entered the store. As the old saying went, this was the first day of the rest of his life. And he was eager to start living. Today was the beginning of something good.

Cal made his way over to the flower display and studied the selection. As he had hoped, there were daffodils and roses, and he chose a dozen of each, pleased with his inside knowledge about flowers and their meaning. Daffodils for Isobel to celebrate her new beginning. Red and white roses for Abby to show honorable admiration.

Well, maybe a bit more than admiration. If he was feeling brave.

Tucking the bouquets under his arm, he hobbled up to the cash register at the front of the store. Kelly Kay, an acquaintance from church, was the clerk on duty, and she greeted him with a wide smile.

"Sheriff! I'm so glad to see you up and about. It was all everyone was talking about after early-morning service. We were shocked to hear about poor Isobel delivering her baby in the back room of the bank. And you and Abby and the baby on the run from kidnappers. But thank the Lord that you all made it out alive. We're all praying for you and Abby."

"Thanks, Kelly. I'm always grateful to receive extra prayers, and the Lord was sure listening."

"I heard that the bomb squad was still at the bank this morning?" The statement was phrased as a question as Kelly ran his credit card through the machine.

He bit back a chuckle. Apparently, the rumor mill was operating at full force. "Yes, indeed. We had to call in the boys from Fargo to help remove the explosives. But it's all clear now. It'll be back to business as usual by Monday."

A relieved expression washed over her face as she handed him the receipt. "Well, I might be presuming too much, but I hope you'll give Isobel and Abby my best when you see them."

"I will indeed."

Now he just needed to find the location of Isobel and Abby's rooms. He rubbed his jaw as he looked down the hallway for the help desk. His chin felt scruffy and rough beneath his fingers, and he realized just how mangy he must look. A day's worth of stubble had turned his usually well-trimmed goatee into the beginnings of an unkempt beard. If that wasn't bad enough, he was still dressed for ice fishing on the lake, his overalls still flapping in the spot where Abby had ripped them.

He considered heading home to change into something more presentable but decided to seize the moment instead. Abby wouldn't care about his clothes. Not after everything they had been through together.

Noticing a bank of elevators at the end of the right corridor, he pointed his crutches in that direction, hoping the reception desk would be nearby. Sure enough, there it was at the end of the hall.

"Good morning," he said, flashing his badge to a tall, raven-haired woman in a leopard print blouse. "Can you tell me where I can find Abigail Marshall and Isobel Carrolls?"

The young woman's fingers flew across the keyboard of her computer.

"Of course, Sheriff. Let me just see if I can find… Oh, here it is. Isobel Carrolls is in room three-oh-eight." She didn't look up as she scrolled down the screen. "But Abigail Marshall was treated and released a few hours ago."

He nodded his thanks and then headed toward the elevator. He pressed three and closed his eyes as he rode up the two flights to the third floor.

All of a sudden, his heart was just a little less buoyant.

He couldn't help feeling a pang of disappointment, and, if he was being honest, maybe a little hurt. He had thought Abby would have stuck around long enough to make sure he was okay.

But that wasn't fair. She had been through a terrible ordeal and deserved to go home and get some sleep. Plus, she couldn't have known what time he would arrive at the hospital. He had stuck around at the lodge for several hours after the ambulances left, helping the other officers gather evidence from the scene.

He allowed his spirits to lift. He would swing by her house after he visited Isobel.

The elevator shuddered to a stop, and the door opened. A sign directed him to the right, and he swung forward on his crutches and proceeded down the hall.

The door to 308 was slightly ajar, and when he tapped gently, it swung open all the way. Isobel, dressed in a hospital gown, was lying on the bed. Her eyes were closed, and she was snoring softly.

Slumped in the chair next to her was Abby. Also fast asleep.

He pushed the door open wider and leaned in against the frame. Abby's dark hair was pulled to the side, and her face was relaxed in repose. She had a pair of woolen slippers on her feet, and across her shoulders was a jacket with the words PROPERTY OF DAGGER LAKE SHERIFF DEPT stenciled down the sleeve.

As he gazed at her, he could feel his eyes begin to blaze and a flush of warmth curl from his insides. He loved this woman. More than he ever thought possible. With all his heart and soul.

He watched the steady rise and fall of her chest for a few more seconds, feeling his own heart beating in time with her breathing. Both women were exhausted and needed rest, and he didn't want to disturb their slumber. But as he turned to make a quiet exit, he stumbled, and one of the crutches slipped from his grip.

The thud of something falling on to the floor woke Abby with a start. How odd was it that she had been thinking about Cal as she fell asleep? And, the first thing she saw when she opened her eyes was the sheriff himself, standing in the doorway, with two bouquets of flowers in his arms?

Was her heart playing tricks on her brain? She looked around the room and tried to blink away the confusing feeling that she was still a hostage at the bank. In the moment it took for her consciousness to adjust to reality, a kaleidoscope of images tumbled across her brain. Being escorted into the emergency room to be checked for hypothermia and shock. Retrieving a voice mail and hearing the long-awaited news that her adoption petition had been granted and that Davey Lightfoot would be coming to stay with her in a matter of days. That she would have a son. A family. And then, deciding to stay with Isobel in her hospital room. And now, seeing Cal limping toward her with daffodils and roses in his hands.

A smile teased the corners of his mouth as he handed her a cellophane-covered package of flowers. "I was going to bring these to your room, but they told me you had been treated and released. How did you manage that? It must have taken a full dose of Abby Marshall charm to convince the nurses to let you bunk in here with Isobel."

"Thanks for the roses, Cal." She bent to inhale the sweet scent of the bouquet. "What about you? I'm surprised that you aren't a patient yourself, between that bullet wound and the blow you took to the head."

"Shh." He pantomimed holding his finger to his lips. "I forgot to mention how that last part went down." He cast his eyes over to where Isobel was sleeping on the bed. "How's the new mom?"

"She's doing well, considering. The baby passed his initial assessments with flying colors, and that helped a lot. I think she's still worried about Ricky, though. She told me she expects that he'll be out on bail by tonight at the latest."

"That's not going happen." Cal set down his crutches and leaned against the railing of the bed. "There's a whole busload of charges being leveled against him, not the least of which is attempted murder and kidnapping. And my sources tell me that Martina, Max and Tomas are showing signs they might be willing to turn state's evidence as part of a plea deal. Even if they change their minds, we have three extremely reputable eyewitnesses who can testify to their criminal intent. Ricky is not squirming his way out of this one."

At the sound of her husband's name, Isobel awoke

with a start. "What did you say?" Her voice was slurred from sleep, but her face was tense and alert. "Was I dreaming, or were you just talking about Ricky?"

"Hey. How's it going? Where's the little guy?" Cal smiled as he handed her the packet of bright yellow daffodils.

"He's in the nursery," Isobel said. "Apparently, it's standard procedure in cases like this. I'd feel a lot better about letting him out of my sight if I knew for sure that Ricky wasn't about to appear at any moment, asserting his parental rights."

"You don't need to worry about that. Last I heard, Ricky was being transported to Fargo under armed guard. Turns out, he is a very popular man. As soon as the word went out that we had him in custody, calls began pouring in from government agencies across the state. DEA. FBI. BTAF. Everyone wants a piece of him. The deputies at the office even had a surprise visit from a couple of guys from the Bureau of Homeland Security. Rest assured that the feds aren't going to let this one drop. He's going to be behind bars for a very long time."

Isobel's face remained still for a moment, and then she nodded. "Thanks, Cal. That's what I needed to hear. I believe that this time justice will finally be served." She put her hand over her mouth to cover a yawn. "Now, if you two don't mind, I think I better get some sleep before they bring Calvin Marshall Carrolls in for me to nurse."

Abby grinned. "That's a mouthful, but I have to admit that I like the way it sounds."

Cal nodded, his eyes suddenly misty. "I'm honored

to be your son's namesake. It might not be easy for the little guy when he realizes that I'm going to be watching out for him, but that will happen whether he likes it or not." He turned and offered Abby a sidelong glance. "What do you say to taking a walk down to the nursery and looking at baby Carrolls? Even though it's only been a few hours, I'm missing him already."

Abby's heart drummed in her chest as she followed Cal out the door. It was only a stroll along the hospital hallway, but somehow it felt like she was about to embark on something bigger. As the door swished closed behind them, Cal leaned against the wall to catch his breath.

"You okay, Cal?" she asked.

"I'm fine." He shook his head. "I didn't expect to get that emotional back there in the room. And I have to say that little Cal should be honored to have 'Marshall' as his middle name."

"Aww." She pretended to punch his arm. Maybe if she kept it light and jokey Cal wouldn't realize that she was touched by Isobel's gesture, as well.

He shifted his weight on his crutches as they started down the hall. "I don't know what else I could have said to make Isobel feel safe. Her husband is one bad dude. And he's managed to walk before, so I understand her concern. But it's not going to happen this time."

"I think she'll feel better when she gets some sleep," she said, slowing her gait as they approached the over-size window that overlooked the nursery. "But rest might be a hard thing to come by if that little guy has anything to say about it." She pointed at the bassinet with the blue label marked "Carrolls Baby Boy," where a red-faced infant with clenched fists was screaming with all his might. The nurse in charge waved them over to the door.

"Hi, Abby," the older woman greeted her warmly. "I'd ask if you want to hold him, but we just drew a sample of blood for the lab. So, at the moment, he's not a happy camper. As soon as he calms down, I'm going to take him to see his mom."

"That's okay. Cal and I just wanted to stop by and admire the little guy."

The nurse nodded and walked back inside.

Cal eased forward on his crutches and fixed his eyes on the bassinet.

"So," he said, pausing just a moment to adjust his stance. "I've been thinking about it, and I reckon I owe you a couple of overdue apologies. I know that the two of us got off on the wrong foot when I first came to town, and I've never been happy about that.

"I'm sorry for whatever I may have said about Dagger Lake. The truth is, I like living in this town, and I have nothing but respect for its citizens. One, in particular, stands out above the rest. She took on a perp twice her size with a serving tray and delivered a baby in the back room of a bank. Not to mention the fact that she saved my life on more than one occasion. I won't mention any names, but I think you know who I'm talking about."

She could feel herself blushing. She hadn't been expecting such a heartfelt admission. "Well, the feelings go both ways. I should have been more up-front about my attempts to adopt Davey and not left you waiting alone in the restaurant."

A mischievous glint flicked in Cal's eyes. "Now that we've gotten that out of the way, I guess we should talk about that kiss. I suppose I could apologize for that, as well, but I'm just not feeling it. My dad always told me that drastic times call for drastic measures. So, when it hit me that I might die without ever getting to kiss you, that seemed like a pity. And I went for it."

He went for it? That didn't sound romantic. More pragmatic than quixotic. She offered a confused smile. "Okay."

"Right," he said with a brisk nod. There was a moment of silence as they stared through the glass at their namesake.

Cal cleared his throat. "I just realized that I never even asked how you were doing. That final moment with Ricky must have been terrifying."

"I was standing there, praying, and then there you were. I don't think I've ever been so happy to see someone in my entire life. I'm grateful that you found me." She stretched on her tiptoes and kissed his cheek.

His gaze dropped to meet hers, and she hastened to pull back. But his arm was suddenly wrapped around her waist, pulling her into an embrace.

"I had to find you. I love you, Abby," he said.

He loved her. A pang of joy ricocheted through her brain. "I love you, too, Cal. For a moment there, I was afraid that I'd never have the chance to tell you."

He gazed down at her and shook his head. "I never doubted we'd make it through."

"Um… Cal? You do realize that you've just messed up your excuse for stealing that kiss."

He bent to cup her chin in his hand. "So I did," he said with a smile. "I guess I'll have to remember that when I tell the story to our kids."

She pulled back, reality hitting her. Kids. Davey.

Cal gave her a questioning smile. "What's wrong?"

She took a deep breath, but before she could speak, he interrupted her. "I hope you're about to tell me that you already know who our eldest son is going to be."

Happy tears filled her eyes, but she blinked them away. "I finally heard from the agency. The adoption was approved."

Her heart somersaulted as he closed the gap between them. A kiss to mark a new beginning. And a new life together as a family.

EPILOGUE

Cal looked around the restaurant, his heart overflowing with love and gratitude to all his family and friends gathered together today. There was Isobel, chatting with Abby's brother, Gideon, and his wife, Dani, whose baby bump was just beginning to show beneath her flowing dress. Isobel was holding baby Calvin Marshall, who at six months was beginning to roll over and scoot. Looking at the little tyke in his green overalls, grinning and proudly showing off his two teeth, Cal found it hard to believe that he was the same child who had seemed so small and fragile just a few months ago.

Clustered on the other side of the tables were his four sisters who had arrived earlier in the week with their families in tow. His nieces and nephews were currently chasing one another around the private dining room, dodging through chairs and the other guests, while his brothers-in-law stood behind their wives, monitoring the children. In theory, at least. His own parents were in the corner, deep in conversation with his former police captain from Saint Cloud and Mayor Hovland. They all seemed to have quite a lot to say.

His eyes continued to scan the crowd. Was that Mr. Ratten beside Linette? And the entire paramedic squad still wearing their uniforms? Between Abby's extended family, coworkers and friends, it seemed as if almost all of Dagger Lake was squeezed into the pizzeria. The only one missing was Abby's mother. Abby and Gideon had tried to talk her into attending, but she had dismissed the invitation, claiming she had something better to do.

"Tomorrow's the big day, huh?" A hand clapped him on the back.

Cal turned around to see Gideon, Abby's younger brother. "I had to break away from the females. Isobel and Dani have begun comparing pregnancy notes and discussing the best baby food and when to start introducing solids. I say, let's just wait until the little guy arrives before we worry about what we're feeding him."

Cal smiled at Gideon's comment. Gideon might pretend to be uninterested in his wife's condition, but he knew full well that his friend was overjoyed at the prospect of becoming a dad.

"Speaking of females," Gideon continued, "where is that sister of mine? She owes me a dance tonight before I give her away tomorrow."

"Thanks again for doing that," Cal said. He understood and appreciated the significance of Gideon's role in the ceremony and why it was so important for Abby to have her brother walk her down the aisle. For a long time, it had been just the two of them taking care of each other. And it was right and proper that Gideon should stand in the place of their father.

"The thing is, she was the one who always looked out for me. She had to play Mom and Dad as well as provider when she was still just a kid." Gideon brushed the back of his hand against his eye, pushing back some mistiness. "I'm glad she found you. It's time that there was someone to finally take care of Abby."

"You know that I'll always do my best by her." Cal's voice sounded thick to his own ears. If he couldn't get through tonight, how was he ever going to make it through tomorrow?

"Didn't I tell you?" Gideon jabbed him in the ribs. "I always knew that you and my sis would make a good team."

Too true. All the matchmakers had been proven right.

"There's my sister." Gideon pointed across the room. "I'm going to go and claim some time before you come in and steal her away."

Cal watched as Gideon walked toward Abby, who was standing by the buffet, talking to one of the servers. His breath hitched as Abby turned and caught his stare. She was so beautiful. Her dark hair hung loose down past her shoulders, skimming the top of her ivory sundress. Her mouth formed a warm smile as she gave a little wave in his direction before turning toward her brother and pulling him into a tight embrace.

How could God have blessed him so abundantly? Cal felt humbled and unworthy when he thought back to the many gifts that God had granted in the days and weeks following the bank heist and failed kidnapping. There was, of course, the health and well-being of Isobel and her baby. It still struck him as amazing that Abby had delivered little Calvin Marshall in the break room of the bank and that the newborn had withstood a trek through a blizzard, a treacherous ride on a sled and a snowmobile, not to mention a couple of narrow escapes. And yet somehow God kept him safe from harm.

But there would be no happy ending for Isobel's now-ex-husband, Ricky. Cal made it a point to keep tabs on the case, and the last he heard, Max and Martina were negotiating a plea deal, agreeing to testify against their boss on the charges of attempted murder and kidnapping. And now Isobel would no longer have to fear the long shadow of Ricky as she struggled to make a new life for herself and her son.

Blessings abounded. And then there was Davey. Abby's application had been granted and Davey had been able to move out of the temporary shelter and into Abby's home a few days after their escape. The adoption had been made official just last month. And tomorrow Davey would stand beside him as the best man in their wedding. It was only right that the little boy would play a major role in the ceremony since he was such an essential part of their life. Right now, he was legally Abby's son. But the day after the wedding, Cal would be filing his own petition to the court to formally adopt Davey as well. The papers were already drawn up, and he had explained to Davey how much he wanted to be his father in name as well as deed.

His eyes skimmed across the crowd of family and friends, looking for the little boy. Although Davey had adjusted well to life with Abby, he sometimes retreated into himself when he felt overwhelmed. A large gathering like this was just the type of situation that might cause him to slip away into a quiet corner for a moment of solitude.

Cal circled back around the restaurant, but there was no sign of Davey anywhere. A jolt of anxiety crashed through his veins. Where could the little boy be? He had seen him less than fifteen minutes earlier over by the counter, lining up for dessert. Wait a minute. The toe of a familiar, navy blue Croc peeked out from under the table. Cal lifted the white cloth covering and checked underneath. And there was Davey, finishing off a crumbly piece of chocolate cake.

"How are you doing, buddy?" he said, scooting down on his knees to join him under the table.

"Pretty good." The little boy licked the last of the icing off his fingers and shrugged. "But I keep thinking about what I'm supposed to wear tomorrow to the wedding."

"Your tuxedo? What about it?"

Davey frowned. "It makes me look like a penguin."

Cal hid the smile forming on his lips. "I never thought of that. But I'm wearing the same thing, so I suppose I'll be looking like a penguin, too."

"Sheriff and Davey Penguin." An arm twined around his waist as Abby slid next to them on the floor. "I kind of like the sound of it."

Davey nodded, his eyes serious. "Yeah. I guess it's okay since Cal and I are going to match. I'm still a little hungry. Is it okay if I get another piece of cake?"

"Just a small one." Abby smiled at the little boy as he pushed himself up from the floor and watched as

Davey walked over to the buffet table at the other end of the room. She then turned to Cal. "This time tomorrow, we'll be husband and wife. Can you believe it?"

Believe it? He'd only been waiting the last six months for this moment.

"It's about time," he growled back, his lips grazing her jaw in a quick kiss.

Abby laughed and pulled away. "Your family is wonderful. I can't believe so many people came out for the rehearsal dinner."

"So much for limiting it to family and out-of-town guests," Cal pretended to grumble. "Now I'm starting to worry that we won't have enough food for tomorrow."

"Oh, there'll be plenty," Abby said. "How did your fishing expedition go this morning?"

"Well, Davey and my dad were the only ones who caught anything. And they sure enjoyed rubbing it in." Cal laughed, remembering the boy's look of surprise and pride when Davey had reeled in the first catch of the day. "I snapped a couple pictures of the two of them showing off their success."

A warmth spread across his chest as he thought back to his "bachelor" party of a few hours ago. The men in the two families had woken up while it was still dark, trekked down to the lake and then hung their rods in the water and watched the sunrise. How unbelievable to think that just a few months ago he had planned to go ice fishing and ended up locked inside the bank with Abby instead. He hadn't caught any walleye or perch that weekend, either.

No. Instead he'd snagged something so much better.

And there was going to be no catch and release. He'd finally found the woman of his dreams and the family he had always hoped for.

* * * * *

If you enjoyed Rescue on the Run,
*pick up these other thrilling stories
from Jaycee Bullard:*

Framed for Christmas
Fatal Ranch Reunion

Available now from Love Inspired Suspense!

Find more great reads at www.LoveInspired.com

Dear Reader,

Thank you for joining me on a journey that has been very near and dear to my heart since Abby and Cal made their first appearance in my debut LIS book, *Framed for Christmas*. I knew as soon as I wrote that short bit of banter between the crabby sheriff and no-nonsense paramedic that these two feisty characters had a story to tell. And, indeed they did. This has been my very favorite book to write; but it was also the hardest to plot and frame. I owe endless thanks to my editor, Dina, for her guidance and support through the multiple drafts and revisions! I hope you enjoyed spending time with Cal and Abby as much as I enjoyed telling their tale!

I love hearing from my readers. You can contact me on Facebook at https://www.facebook.com/jaycee.bullard.1 or Instagram at https://www.instagram.com/jceebullard/?hl=en.

Jaycee Bullard

**WE HOPE YOU ENJOYED
THIS BOOK FROM**

LOVE INSPIRED SUSPENSE

INSPIRATIONAL ROMANCE

Courage. Danger. Faith.

Find strength and determination in stories
of faith and love in the face of danger.

6 NEW BOOKS AVAILABLE EVERY MONTH!

LISHALO2021

HARLEQUIN

Uplifting or passionate,
heartfelt or thrilling—
Harlequin has your
happily-ever-after.

With a wide range of romance series that each
offer new books every month, you are sure to
find the satisfying escape you deserve.

Look for all Harlequin series
new releases on the
***last Tuesday* of each month**
in stores and online!

Harlequin.com

HONSALE0521

COMING NEXT MONTH FROM
Love Inspired Suspense

ARCTIC WITNESS
Alaska K-9 Unit • by Heather Woodhaven
When his ex-wife goes missing in the Alaskan wilderness after discovering a body, Alaska State Trooper Sean West and his K-9 partner, Grace, rescue her from a kidnapper. Now the murderer is on their trail, and it's up to Sean to protect Ivy and the little boy she plans to adopt.

MOUNTAIN FUGITIVE
by Lynette Eason
Out on a horseback ride, Dr. Kathrine Gilroy stumbles into the middle of a shoot-out. Now US Marshal Dominic O'Ryan injured and under her care, she's determined to help him find the fugitive who killed his partner...before they both end up dead.

COVERT AMISH INVESTIGATION
Amish Country Justice • by Dana R. Lynn
Police officer Kate Bontrager never planned to return to her Amish roots, but with a woman missing from witness protection in Kate's former community, she has no choice. The moment she arrives for her undercover assignment, she becomes a target...and working with her ex, Abram Burkholder, is her only hope of staying alive.

HIGH STAKES ESCAPE
Mount Shasta Secrets • by Elizabeth Goddard
Someone is killing off deputy US Marshal Ben Bradley's witnesses one by one, and he won't let Chasey Cook become the next victim. But on the run with a leak in the Marshals Service and murderers drawing closer, he and Chasey have no one to trust. Can he shield her from danger on his own?

KIDNAP THREAT
by Anne Galbraith
A mole in the police department thrusts a witness's mother right into a deadly gang's crosshairs. They'll kill anyone to keep Alice Benoit's son from testifying. Now it's up to officer Ben Parsons to protect Alice for twenty-four hours in a busy city...or a killer could go free.

SNOWSTORM SABOTAGE
by Kerry Johnson
After single mom Everly Raven finds her friend murdered inside a chalet on her family's ski resort, the blame falls on her. With a blizzard closing in and the killer's henchmen chasing her down a mountain, Everly must work with FBI agent Isaac Rhodes—the father of her secret child—to clear her name.

LOOK FOR THESE AND OTHER LOVE INSPIRED BOOKS WHEREVER BOOKS ARE SOLD, INCLUDING MOST BOOKSTORES, SUPERMARKETS, DISCOUNT STORES AND DRUGSTORES.

LISCNM0921

Get 4 FREE REWARDS!

We'll send you 2 FREE Books plus 2 FREE Mystery Gifts.

Love Inspired Suspense books showcase how courage and optimism unite in stories of faith and love in the face of danger.

FREE
Value Over
$20

YES! Please send me 2 FREE Love Inspired Suspense novels and my 2 FREE mystery gifts (gifts are worth about $10 retail). After receiving them, if I don't wish to receive any more books, I can return the shipping statement marked "cancel." If I don't cancel, I will receive 6 brand-new novels every month and be billed just $5.24 each for the regular-print edition or $5.99 each for the larger-print edition in the U.S., or $5.74 each for the regular-print edition or $6.24 each for the larger-print edition in Canada. That's a savings of at least 13% off the cover price. It's quite a bargain! Shipping and handling is just 50¢ per book in the U.S. and $1.25 per book in Canada.* I understand that accepting the 2 free books and gifts places me under no obligation to buy anything. I can always return a shipment and cancel at any time. The free books and gifts are mine to keep no matter what I decide.

Choose one:
☐ **Love Inspired Suspense Regular-Print** (153/353 IDN GNWN)

☐ **Love Inspired Suspense Larger-Print** (107/307 IDN GNWN)

Name (please print)

Address   Apt. #

City   State/Province   Zip/Postal Code

Email: Please check this box ☐ if you would like to receive newsletters and promotional emails from Harlequin Enterprises ULC and its affiliates. You can unsubscribe anytime.

Mail to the **Harlequin Reader Service:**
IN U.S.A.: P.O. Box 1341, Buffalo, NY 14240-8531
IN CANADA: P.O. Box 603, Fort Erie, Ontario L2A 5X3

Want to try 2 free books from another series! Call 1-800-873-8635 or visit www.ReaderService.com.

---

*Terms and prices subject to change without notice. Prices do not include sales taxes, which will be charged (if applicable) based on your state or country of residence. Canadian residents will be charged applicable taxes. Offer not valid in Quebec. This offer is limited to one order per household. Books received may not be as shown. Not valid for current subscribers to Love Inspired Suspense books. All orders subject to approval. Credit or debit balances in a customer's account(s) may be offset by any other outstanding balance owed by or to the customer. Please allow 4 to 6 weeks for delivery. Offer available while quantities last.

Your Privacy—Your information is being collected by Harlequin Enterprises ULC, operating as Harlequin Reader Service. For a complete summary of the information we collect, how we use this information and to whom it is disclosed, please visit our privacy notice located at corporate.harlequin.com/privacy-notice. From time to time we may also exchange your personal information with reputable third parties. If you wish to opt out of this sharing of your personal information, please visit readerservice.com/consumerschoice or call 1-800-873-8635. **Notice to California Residents**—Under California law, you have specific rights to control and access your data. For more information on these rights and how to exercise them, visit corporate.harlequin.com/california-privacy.

LIS21R2